FIGH

Mostly to do with school and all to do with children, these stories explore a secret world of feelings and inner conflicts we all know well.

'Cheating' deals with guilt over cheating in a maths test, 'One Good Turn' with hating your best friend and thumping her, and 'Marmaduke' with making up an imaginary friend who takes the blame for everything that goes wrong!

All young readers will find something to identify with in this collection of perceptive, warm and funny stories by twelve talented and well-known writers.

FIGHTING
IN BREAK
and other stories

Edited by
Barbara Ireson

Illustrated by Susan Hellard

PUFFIN BOOKS
in association with Faber and Faber

PUFFIN BOOKS

Published by the Penguin Group
27 Wrights Lane, London W8 5TZ, England
Viking Penguin Inc., 40 West 23rd Street, New York, New York 10010, USA
Penguin Books Australia Ltd, Ringwood, Victoria, Australia
Penguin Books Canada Ltd, 2801 John Street, Markham, Ontario, Canada L3R 1B4
Penguin Books (NZ) Ltd, 182–190 Wairau Road, Auckland 10, New Zealand

Penguin Books Ltd, Registered Offices: Harmondsworth, Middlesex, England

First published by Faber and Faber Limited 1987
Published in Puffin Books 1989
1 3 5 7 9 10 8 6 4 2

Printed and bound in Great Britain by
Cox & Wyman Ltd, Reading
Filmset in Palatino

Acknowledgements

The editor is grateful for permission to use the following
copyright material:

Hey, Danny! by Robin Klein, by permission of Curtis
Brown (Aust.) Pty. Ltd.

The Dinner Lady Who Made Magic by Dorothy Edwards
from *The Cat-flap and the Apple Pie,* edited by Lance Salway,
published by W. H. Allen. Copyright © 1979 the Dorothy
Edwards Trust

The Balaclava Story from *A Northern Childhood: The Balaclava
Story and other Stories* by George Layton (published in
Longman Knockouts series) by permission of Longman

Fighting in Break from *Nicholas and the Gang Again* by René
Goscinny, by permission of the Blackie Publishing Group
and Les Editions Denoel

Cheating from *Family Secrets* by Susan Shreve. Copyright ©
1979 by Susan Shreve. Reprinted by permission of Alfred
A. Knopf Inc. and Russell & Volkening as agents for the
author

Contents

Hey, Danny!
Robin Klein

'Right,' said Danny's mother sternly. 'That school bag cost ten dollars. You can just save up your pocket money to buy another one. How could you possibly lose a big school bag, anyhow?'

'Dunno,' said Danny. 'I just bunged in some empty bottles to take back to the milkbar, and I was sort of swinging it round by the handles coming home, and it sort of fell over that culvert thing down on to a truck on the freeway.'

'And you forgot to write your name and phone number in it as I told you to,' said Mrs Hillerey. 'Well, you'll just have to use my blue weekend bag till you save up enough pocket money to replace the old one. And no arguments!'

Danny went and got the blue bag from the hall cupboard and looked at it.

The bag was not just blue; it was a vivid, clear, electric blue, like a flash of lightning. The regulation colour for school bags at his school was a

1

khaki-olive-brown, inside and out, which didn't show stains from when your can of Coke leaked, or when you left your salami sandwiches uneaten and forgot about them for a month.

'I can't take this bag to school,' said Danny. 'Not one this colour. Can't I take my books and stuff in one of those green plastic garbage bags?'

'Certainly not!' said Mrs Hillerey.

On Monday at the bus stop, the kids all stared at the blue bag.

'Hey,' said Jim, who was supposed to be his mate. 'That looks like one of those bags girls take to ballet classes.'

'Hey, Danny, you got one of those frilly dresses in there?' asked Spike.

'Aw, belt up, can't you?' said Danny miserably. On the bus the stirring increased as more and more of the kids got on. It was a very long trip for Danny. It actually took only twenty minutes – when you had an ordinary brown school bag and not a great hunk of sky to carry round with you. Every time anyone spoke to him they called him 'Little Boy Blue'.

'It matches his lovely blue eyes,' said one kid.

'Maybe he's got a little blue trike with training wheels too,' said another kid.

'Hey, Danny, why didn't you wear some nice blue ribbons in your hair?'

When Danny got off the bus he made a dash for his classroom and shoved the bag under his desk. First period they had Miss Reynolds, and when she was marking the roll she looked along the aisle and saw Danny's bag and said, 'That's a very elegant bag you have there, Danny.'

Everyone else looked around and saw the blue bag and began carrying on. Danny kept a dignified silence, and after five minutes Miss Reynolds made them stop singing 'A Life on the Ocean Waves'. But all through Maths and English, heads kept turning round to grin at Danny and his radiantly blue bag.

At morning recess he sneaked into the art room and mixed poster paints into a shade of khaki-olive-brown which he rubbed over his bag with his hankie. When the bell rang he had a grey handkerchief, but the bag was still a clear and innocent blue. 'Darn thing,' Danny muttered in disgust. 'Must be made of some kind of special waterproof atomic material. Nothing sticks to it.'

'What are you doing in the art room, Daniel?' asked Miss Reynolds. 'And what is that terrible painty mess?'

'I was just painting a Zodiac sign on my bag,' said Danny.

'I wish you boys wouldn't write things all over your good school bags. Clean up that mess, Danny, and go to your next class.'

But Danny said he was feeling sick and could he please lie down in the sick bay for a while. He sneaked his blue bag in with him, and found the key to the first-aid box and looked inside for something that would turn bright blue bags brown. There was a little bottle of brown lotion, so Danny tipped the whole lot on to cotton wool and scrubbed it into the surface of the bag. But the lotion just ran off the bag and went all over his hands and the bench top in the sick bay.

'Danny Hillerey!' said the school secretary. 'You know very well that no student is allowed to unlock the first-aid box. What on earth are you doing?'

'Sorry,' said Danny. 'Just looking for fruit salts.'

'I think you'd better sit quietly out in the fresh air if you feel sick,' Mrs Adams said suspiciously.

'And who owns that peculiar-looking blue bag?'

'It belongs in the sport equipment shed,' said Danny. 'It's got measuring tapes and stuff in it. Blue's our house colour.'

He went and sat outside with the bag shoved under the seat and looked at it and despaired. Kids from his class started going down to the oval for sport, and someone called out, 'It's a beautiful blue, but it hasn't a hood.'

Danny glared and said, 'Get lost' and 'Drop dead.' Then Miss Reynolds came along and made him go down to the oval with the others.

On the way there Danny sloshed the blue bag in a puddle of mud – but nothing happened, the blue became shinier if anything. He also tried grass stains under the sprinkler, which had the same effect. Amongst the line-up of khaki-olive-brown bags, his blue one was as conspicuous as a Clydesdale horse in a herd of small ponies.

'Hey, Danny, what time's your tap dancing lesson?' said the kids.

'Hey, Danny, where did you get that knitting bag? I want to buy one for my Aunty.'

'Hey, Danny, when did you join the Bluebell marching girls' squad?'

Finally Danny had had enough.

'This bag's very valuable if you want to know,' he said.

'Garn,' everyone scoffed. 'It's just an ordinary old vinyl bag.'

'I had to beg my Mum to let me bring that bag to school,' said Danny. 'It took some doing, I can tell you. Usually she won't let it out of the house.'

'Why?' demanded everyone. 'What's so special about it?'

Danny grabbed back his bag and wiped off the traces of mud and poster paint and ulcer lotion and grass stains. The bag was stained inside where all that had seeped in through the seams and the zipper, and it would take some explaining when his mother noticed it. (Which she would, next time she went to spend the weekend at Grandma's.) There was her name inside it, E. Hillerey, in big neat letters. E for Enid.

'Well,' said Danny, 'that bag belongs to . . .

Well, if you really want to know, it went along on that expedition up Mount Everest.'

Everyone jeered.

'It did so,' said Danny. 'Look, Sir Edmund Hillary, there's his name printed right there inside. And there's a reason it's this funny colour. So it wouldn't get lost in the snow. It was the bag Sir Edmund Hillary carried that flag in they stuck up on top of Mount Everest. But I'm not going to bring it to school any more if all you can do is poke fun at the colour.'

Everyone went all quiet and respectful.

'Gee,' said Jeff in an awed voice, and he touched the letters that Danny's mother had written with a laundry marking pencil.

'Gosh,' said Mark. 'We never knew you were related to that Sir Edmund Hillary.'

Danny looked modest. 'We're only distantly related,' he admitted. 'He's my Dad's second cousin.'

'Hey, Danny, can I hold it on the bus? I'll be real careful with it.'

'Hey, Danny, can I have a turn when you bring it to school tomorrow?'

'I'll charge you ten cents a go,' said Danny. 'That's fair, for a bag that went up to the top of Mount Everest.'

'Ten cents a kid,' he calculated. 'One hundred kids at ten cents a turn, ten dollars. A new brown school bag. And with a bit of luck, I'll earn all that

7

before someone checks up in the library and finds out Sir Edmund Hillary's name's spelled differently!'

The Dinner Lady Who Made Magic
Dorothy Edwards

Frogover Road Primary School is housed in an old and ugly building. It has windows that are too high to look out of, a yard like iron that you daren't fall down on, bogs that always need plumbing, and more wild kids than good books. There is so much noise coming in from outside, where there is a busy road one way and a railway line the other, that it is murder when the windows have to be wedged open in summer. In winter, when the windows are shut tight, it is like hell, getting hotter and hotter all the time. There was a time when the boilers that clattered and bumbled from below sounded as if they were just going to blow up. That was the time when the school was a pretty dreadful place to be in.

In those days, the Frogover Road kids were a really nasty lot. They pinched one another's dinner money to buy stink bombs to drop at Assembly, they wrote rude things about the teachers in school chalk on the outside walls and blamed other people when they were caught, and they told lies and used swear words and few of them ever spoke below a shout.

The tough kids were always making new gangs and busting up the old ones and, when that happened, there'd be blacks and whites and Asians and Chinese and Cypriots and Arabs all mixed up, bashing each other up and down the playground and over the classrooms; boys and girls punching and clawing, teachers yelling and screaming at them to stop, and the little tiddlers in the Reception class crying and wanting to go home. As for the kids who weren't tough – they'd just keep out of everyone's way as much as possible, and pretend to read books with their fingers in their ears. The only thing no one ever did at that school was learn anything.

At dinner-time, the dinner ladies were as cross as two sticks: they dunked out the potatoes and sloshed the stew and pushed out the plates of prunes and custard without looking anyone in the face, and as soon as another job came their way, they gave in their notices at once. And the children were so horrible and the teachers so bad-tempered that no one even noticed when they went.

And it might have gone on like that: on and on for ever and ever, getting worse and worse, if it hadn't been for a bit of magic.

Now, you'd never have believed that any kind of magic would have been likely to find its way into that part of London. All those miserable, treacherous pavements with the cracks and dips in them, and the houses with several families jammed together under one roof, and the shops with windows full of ugly posters, and the old men who spat at the street corners. 'Magic?' you'd have said. 'Why, even the colour tellies in the hire-shop windows aren't magic any more – everyone has them now.'

But there *was* a bit of magic all right. It came over from the West Indies with a boy called Gerry's grandmam. This boy called Gerry's grandmam flew over for a visit one summer and man, was *she* something special? She was a real witch. Nothing creepy or turning you into something horrible if you upset her or anything – just an old black lady who was good at spells. She knew about things: what spices to mix together, the right knots to tie in pig's chitterlings, how many black chicken's feathers to burn at one go and why you couldn't brew spells over a gas-ring – things like that. Mild stuff for making the odd friendly spell.

Gerry's grandmam was so black that she shone, and so fat that she walked with a bounce like an air-balloon, and so kind that the meanest, crossest check-out girl in the dingiest supermarket had to smile with her. And when she laughed, which she often did, her chuckles gurgled and bubbled like a Lakeland beck and everyone around her laughed to hear her.

Now, around the time Gerry's grandmam was over, there was a crisis at Frogover Road, a *serious* crisis – a walk-out. There had been trouble in the dinner-hour, real trouble. It had started when a girl called Lucy Wilkins, who had yellow hair with green slides in it, had pushed in front of a girl called Carmen Melinski and tried to take her place in the dinner queue.

Lucy was a big 'I'm-the-boss-lady-around-here' sort of girl, with a strong gang behind her, who liked and expected to be treated as Queen of the School. Carmen was a new girl, little and

12

quiet, with black hair and deep blue eyes and very red lips, who looked like she couldn't blow fluff off a milkshake. No one had expected Carmen to be anything but meek, but instead, quick as a flash, Carmen's olive fingers dug themselves into Lucy's gold mop, the green slides skittered to the floor, Lucy fell hard against Horace Loss, a pale-brown West Indian with long eyelashes and a quick temper, and before you could say 'battle' they were all at it. Mashed potato flew across the hall, creamed carrots slithered beneath the struggling bodies and custard dripped from the table-tops. And then five terrified little first-years, running for refuge among the alarmed dinner ladies, upset the fish fingers on to the stove and set them alight!

If the school secretary hadn't phoned at once for the police and the fire brigade, someone might have been killed. The hot, food-plastered children stood in disgraced rows while first the police sergeant, then the fire chief and then the Headmistress gave them good tellings-off. By rights they should have been sent home in disgrace but, as most of their mothers were working, they'd have nowhere to go and might have got into more trouble. So there they had to stay, dinner-bedecked and depressed, until it was time for school to finish for the day. The only ones who went home, at once and for ever, were the angry dinner ladies, who resigned in a bunch.

'And now what shall we do?' the school secretary asked the Headmistress.

The Headmistress rang the Chief Education Officer. 'What *shall* we do about dinners in future for Frogover Primary? We can manage with one lady short if we have to, but not the lot. Oh, my!'

But all the Chief Education Officer could say was, 'Advertise, advertise!'

So, whether they liked it or not, the best that could be done for Frogover Road's midday meal was bread and cheese and apples, which made the kids mutinous and their parents ask what they were supposed to be paying for. But what else could be done? Dinner ladies don't grow on trees! The word had gone round and so, in spite of the advertisements that the Headmistress put in the local paper, and the ones that the school secretary placed on the paper-shop boards, and in spite of the phone calls to the Job Centre, no one wanted to work in a school with a reputation as bad as Frogover Road's.

So it went on being bread and cheese cut into lumps by the overworked secretary, and specky apples from the market, and no one daring to grumble aloud because they knew they'd gone too far. What with that Carmen Melinski behaving like a smug mouse, and a thankful gang of previously persecuted nonentities going home in a posse, and Lucy Wilkins, with sticking plaster down the side of her face where she had been scratched, smouldering in the middle of her lot, and Horace Loss and his mates sulking all playtime down by the dustbins, and Achmed, Shemsha and Mouki and their crowd going off into corners and whispering, it's a wonder that the secretary didn't walk out too.

But she was a nice lady – worried, but nice. The kids quite liked her. One or two of the better-natured ones even felt sorry for her, sorry enough to help with the cheese-cutting. But of course it couldn't go on. The situation was explosive.

The third morning after the walk-out of the dinner ladies, while she was waiting at Tesco's check-out with a trolley full of cut loaves and cheese, the harassed school secretary looked across at the queue opposite and saw a face. If the sun had been black, that was how it would have beamed! Springy grey curls under a hat like a crown of coloured veils bobbed and nodded above a broad and all-encompassing smile.

'Don' look so down, secretary Miss,' said Gerry's grandmam, who knew the secretary by sight, for wasn't her grandson a second-year Frogover Roader? 'Seems to me now those children have been punished enough. Too much misery can lead to real bad doings. It's time something nice happened in that miserable old school for a change.'

They met as soon as they had passed through

15

the check-outs and the school secretary told Gerry's grandmam what was in her heart: all about how old the school was and how crowded and noisy, how the teachers were edgy and how there wasn't even a proper dining-room, only the assembly hall with temporary tables down the middle. 'It's not the children, really,' she said. 'It's Things. But you can't blame the dinner ladies either,' she went on. 'Those children were very, very naughty. Do you know, the caretaker says that little bits of dried potato are still dropping off the light bulbs?'

Gerry's grandmam listened, and then she laughed, so that the secretary laughed too, and so did the other shoppers, and even the passers-by in the High Street who couldn't hear through the glass found themselves smiling as they hurried by.

'I'm having a fine holiday in this old UK,' the witch-grandmam said. 'I've been to Brighton, and Buckingham Palace, the Commonwealth Institute and the Oval and to visit my sister and her family in Birmingham. But I ain't never been in a school. So, I'll tell you what, I'll come and help with those dinners for a week or two before I fly home again. That *will* be something to talk about when I get back! And I'll look around and find a couple or so other folk to help me.'

And that's what happened. That evening Gerry's grandmam went down to the fried chicken take-away and talked to a couple of rather

posh little old white sister-ladies who were
waiting for potato fritters, and somehow these
old ladies found themselves offering to help out
as dinner ladies.

'It's an emergency – like in the war-time,' said
one. 'I remember making cocoa for the air raid
wardens.'

'We must do our bit for the children,' said the
other, and they giggled with pleasure.

Gerry's grandmam knew a girl called Winnie
Wong, who sat about all day painting her nails,
so she called and asked her if she'd like to help in
the school kitchen as a change from nail-painting
and idling. And, although she'd never meant to,
somehow Winnie Wong found herself saying,
'Yes, all right.'

'Three good helpers will be enough, I guess,'
that old witch-grandmam said.

That night Gerry's grandmam got busy in the
small trodden yard behind the house where
Gerry's family lived. On a black skillet over a fire
of wood-chips she frizzled feathers and burned
spices and whispered spells as old as Africa.
With a long iron spoon she stirred and mashed
the growing magic, turning it over and over to
ensure that every bit received its appropriate
incantation, until the fire died and fell away to
white ash, and the skillet cooled and all that
remained was a bare spoonful of glittery powder.

Next morning at nine o'clock the new dinner

helpers arrived: Gerry's grandmam in her magnificent hat and a flowing overall patterned with birds of paradise, the pale old sisters in frilly pink aprons with streamers that had once been worn by a long-ago parlourmaid, and Winnie Wong in the dark blue trousers and tunic of a Chinese worker, with a red carnation tucked behind her ear for luck. There they were, all ready to heat and dish up the school dinners.

For the first time for days a good warm smell rose up from the kitchen and penetrated the classrooms. That day the Central Kitchen had delivered stew, which now bubbled over the gas-rings.

'Hi-yee-ah,' said Gerry's grandmam as she raised the heavy lids and looked down upon the mutton and vegetables. 'Hi-yee-ah,' she said again, and a pinch of something small and glittery and magic slipped from the end of her wooden spoon and was lost to sight as she stirred the pot.

In the meantime, one of the posh old ladies and Winnie Wong put up the tables and arranged the chairs, while the other sister popped out to the market and came back with a couple of bunches of pink daisies, which she divided out into empty milk bottles and put on each table. 'There!' she said. 'The children will like those!'

The Frogover kids came eagerly to dinner, their noses twitching. For them, they were fairly quiet. There was a hushed feeling in the air and, as they fell into line, they spoke in whispers.

Gerry's grandmam in her rainbow hat served up the mouth-watering stew and beamed as each child carried its plate to where Miss Wong waited, her beautiful fluttering pale hands with their painted nails poised to spoon out the mash and lay it delicately and deliciously beside the meat and veg.

The little old ladies, twittering and tottering, wandered round with fresh jugs of water and helped the little ones to cut their meat and offered cubes of bread like dear old-fashioned grannies, speaking so politely in their posh soft voices that the startled children spoke softly if not poshly back.

And, as they ate, the magic worked; it sank into angry stomachs and soothed and petted them into kindness. Querulous teachers suddenly hushed and smiled at each other. Lucy Wilkins peeled off the sticking plaster which she'd only been wearing for effect – for the marks of Carmen's nails had healed days before – and, rolling it neatly, dropped it in her pocket. Horace Loss and his mates, who had recently formed themselves into the Horseshoe Gang, rose as one boy and, without being asked, collected the empty plates of the Reception class and fetched the helpings of jam roll to save the little things from having to queue. And the Asian children, who were mostly vegetarians, smiled at everyone for, although they had not tasted the stew themselves, the magic working away inside everyone else had created a friendliness they were only too pleased to share.

After dinner, Gerry's grandmam and her helpers washed up and stacked away the dishes, singing happily together. The blended voices of the witch-grandmam, the posh old ladies and the lovely Winnie Wong filled the school as pleasantly as the scent of the midday stew and the kids and the teachers smiled as they listened, and then went on with the lessons in the smoothest way imaginable.

So, day after day, until it was time for her to fly home, Gerry's grandmam and her helpers served the school dinners, dispensing magic until the miserable old building became bright and colourful, the outside noises sounded as pleasant as early-morning bird songs, and the rumbles of the downstairs boiler seemed like the drowsy chuckles of a slumbering giant. Now the school was talked about as a place in a million. Somewhere where it was good to be. Somewhere where the kids liked learning and the teachers liked teaching.

News of its transformation spread through the neighbourhood. In a body, just as they had walked out, the dinner ladies returned to plead for their old jobs back. By now the magic had truly worked. It had penetrated every crack and cranny of the old school building and soaked into the hearts of all who entered it. The Headmistress knew that it would soon be time for Gerry's grandmam to go back home, and that the posh old sisters would be leaving to join the WVS, and that Winnie Wong was soon to marry Mr Ah Foo from the Chinese diner, and so she graciously welcomed the dinner ladies back. And now, so good were the children and so pleasant the teachers, that the dinner ladies found themselves beaming as they dished out the dinners.

Before she left, Gerry's grandmam gave the chief dinner lady a small tinful of magic. 'Just drop a bit in now and again,' she said. 'You may as well use it up.'

But the chief dinner lady didn't believe in spells and she threw the tin away the next day. It didn't really matter, though, for the magic had done its work and goes on making things better and better. When the time comes for those kids to grow up and make their own lives among those old streets and houses, they'll have so much magic in them that they'll make the place a paradise!

The Balaclava Story

George Layton

Tony and Barry both had one. I reckon half the kids in our class had one. But I didn't. My mum wouldn't even listen to me.

'You're not having a balaclava! What do you want a balaclava for in the middle of summer?'

I must've told her about ten times why I wanted a balaclava.

'I want one so's I can join the Balaclava Boys . . .'

'Go and wash your hands for tea, and don't be so silly.'

She turned away from me to lay the table, so I put the curse of the middle finger on her. This was pointing both your middle fingers at somebody when they weren't looking. Tony had started it when Miss Taylor gave him a hundred lines for flicking paper pellets at Jennifer Greenwood. He had to write out a hundred times: 'I must not fire missiles because it is dangerous and liable to cause damage to someone's eye.'

Tony tried to tell Miss Taylor that he hadn't fired a missile, he'd just flicked a paper pellet, but she threw a piece of chalk at him and told him to shut up.

'Don't just stand there – wash your hands.'

'Eh?'

'Don't say "eh", say "pardon".'

'What?'

'Just hurry up, and make sure the dirt comes off in the water, and not on the towel, do you hear?'

Ooh, my mum. She didn't half go on sometimes.

'I don't know what you get up to at school. How do you get so dirty?'

I knew exactly the kind of balaclava I wanted. One just like Tony's, a sort of yellowy-brown. His dad had given it to him because of his earache. Mind you, he didn't like wearing it at first. At school he'd given it to Barry to wear and got it back before home-time. But, all the other lads started asking if they could have a wear of it, so Tony took it back and said from then on nobody but him could wear it, not even Barry. Barry told him he wasn't bothered because he was going to get a balaclava of his own, and so did some of the other lads. And that's how it started – the Balaclava Boys.

It wasn't a gang really. I mean they didn't have meetings or anything like that. They just went around together wearing their balaclavas, and if you didn't have one you couldn't go around with them. Tony and Barry were my best friends, but because I didn't have a balaclava, they wouldn't let me go round with them. I tried.

'Aw, go on, Barry, let us walk round with you.'

'No, you can't. You're not a Balaclava Boy.'

'Aw, go on.'

'No.'

'Please.'

I don't know why I wanted to walk round with them anyway. All they did was wander up and down the playground dressed in their rotten balaclavas. It was daft.

'Go on, Barry, be a sport.'

'I've told you. You're not a Balaclava Boy. You've got to have a balaclava. If you get one, you can join.'

'But I can't, Barry. My mum won't let me have one.'

'Hard luck.'

'You're rotten.'

Then he went off with the others. I wasn't half fed up. All my friends were in the Balaclava Boys. All the lads in my class except me. Wasn't fair. The bell went for the next lesson – ooh heck, handicraft with the Miseryguts Garnett – then it was home-time. All the Balaclava Boys were going in and I followed them.

'Hey, Tony, do you want to go down the

woods after school?'

'No, I'm going round with the Balaclava Boys.'

'Oh.'

Blooming Balaclava Boys. Why wouldn't *my mum* buy *me* a *balaclava*? Didn't she realize that I was losing all my friends, and just because she wouldn't buy me one?

'Eh, Tony, we can go goose-gogging – you know, by those great gooseberry bushes at the other end of the woods.'

'I've told you, I can't.'

'Yes, I know, but I thought you might want to go goose-gogging.'

'Well, I would, but I can't.'

I wondered if Barry would be going as well.

'Is Barry going round with the Balaclava Boys an' all?'

'Course he is.'

'Oh.'

Blooming balaclavas. I wish they'd never been invented.

'Why won't your mum get you one?'

'I don't know. She says it's daft wearing a balaclava in the middle of summer. She won't let me have one.'

'I found mine at home up in our attic.'

Tony unwrapped some chewing-gum and asked me if I wanted a piece.

'No thanks.' I'd've only had to wrap it in my handkerchief once we got in the classroom. You couldn't get away with anything with Mr Garnett.

'Hey, maybe you could find one in your attic.'

For a minute I wasn't sure what he was talking about.

'Find what?'

'A balaclava.'

'No, we haven't even got an attic.'

I didn't half find handicraft class boring. All that mucking about with compasses and rulers. Or else it was weaving, and you got all tangled up with balls of wool. I was just no good at handicraft and Mr Garnett agreed with me. Today was worse than ever. We were painting pictures and we had to call it 'My favourite story'. Tony was painting *Noddy in Toyland*. I told him he'd get into trouble.

'Garnett'll do you.'

'Why? It's my favourite story.'

'Yes, but I don't think he'll believe you.'

Tony looked ever so hurt.

'But honest. It's my favourite story. Anyway what are you doing?'

He leaned over to have a look at my favourite story.

'Have you read it, Tony?'

'I don't know. What is it?'

'It's *Robinson Crusoe*, what do you think it is?'

He just looked at my painting.

'Oh, I see it now. Oh yes, I get it now. I

27

couldn't make it out for a minute. Oh yes, there's Man Friday behind him.'

'Get your finger off, it's still wet. And that isn't Man Friday, it's a coconut tree. And you've smudged it.'

We were using some stuff called poster paint, and I got covered in it. I was getting it everywhere, so I asked Mr Garnett if I could go for a wash. He gets annoyed when you ask to be excused, but he could see I'd got it all over my hands, so he said I could go, but told me to be quick.

The washbasins were in the boys' cloakroom

28

just outside the main hall. I got most of the paint off and as I was drying my hands, that's when it happened. I don't know what came over me. As soon as I saw that balaclava lying there on the floor, I decided to pinch it. I couldn't help it. I just knew that this was my only chance. I've never pinched anything before – I don't think I have – but I didn't think of this as . . . well . . . I don't even like saying it, but . . . well, stealing. I just did it.

I picked it up, went to my coat, and put it in the pocket. At least I tried to put it in the pocket but it bulged out, so I pushed it down the inside of the sleeve. My head was throbbing, and even though I'd just dried my hands, they were all wet from sweating. If only I'd thought a bit first. But it all happened so quickly. I went back to the classroom, and as I was going in I began to realize what I'd done. I'd *stolen* a balaclava. I didn't even know whose it was, but as I stood in the doorway I couldn't believe I'd done it. If only I could go back. In fact I thought I would but then Mr Garnett told me to hurry up and sit down. As I was going back to my desk I felt as if all the lads knew what I'd done. How could they? Maybe somebody had seen me. No! Yes! How *could* they? They could. Of course they couldn't. No, course not. What if they did though? Oh heck.

I thought home-time would never come but when the bell did ring I got out as quick as I

could. I was going to put the balaclava back
before anybody noticed; but as I got to the cloakroom I heard Norbert Lightowler shout out that
someone had pinched his balaclava. Nobody
took much notice, thank goodness, and I heard
Tony say to him that he'd most likely lost it.
Norbert said he hadn't but he went off to make
sure it wasn't in the classroom.

I tried to be all casual and took my coat, but I
didn't dare put it on in case the balaclava popped
out of the sleeve. I said tarah to Tony.

'Tarah, Tony, see you tomorrow.'

'Yeh, tarah.'

Oh, it was good to get out in the open air. I
couldn't wait to get home and get rid of that
blooming balaclava. Why had I gone and done a
stupid thing like that? Norbert Lightowler was
sure to report it to the Headmaster, and there'd
be an announcement about it at morning
Assembly and the culprit would be asked to own
up. I was running home as fast as I could. I
wanted to stop and take out the balaclava and
chuck it away, but I didn't dare. The faster I ran,
the faster my head was filled with thoughts. I
could give it back to Norbert. You know, say I'd
taken it by mistake. No, he'd never believe me.
None of the lads would believe me. Everybody
knew how much I wanted to be a Balaclava Boy.
I'd have to get rid of the blooming thing as fast as
I could.

My mum wasn't back from work when I got home, thank goodness, so as soon as I shut the front door, I put my hand down the sleeve of my coat for the balaclava. There was nothing there. That was funny, I was sure I'd put it down that sleeve. I tried down the other sleeve, and there was still nothing there. Maybe I'd got the wrong coat. No, it was my coat all right. Oh, blimey, I must've lost it while I was running home. I was glad in a way. I was going to have to get rid of it, now it was gone. I only hoped nobody had seen it drop out, but oh, I was glad to be rid of it. Mind you, I was dreading going to school next morning. Norbert'll probably have reported it by now. Well, I wasn't going to own up. I didn't mind the cane, it wasn't that, but if you owned up, you had to go up on the stage in front of the whole school. Well, I was going to forget about it now and nobody would ever know that I'd pinched that blooming lousy balaclava.

I started to do my homework, but I couldn't concentrate. I kept thinking about Assembly next morning. What if I went all red and everybody else noticed? They'd know I'd pinched it then. I tried to think about other things, nice things. I thought about bed. I just wanted to go to sleep. To go to bed and sleep. Then I thought about my mum; what she'd say if she knew I'd been stealing. But I still couldn't forget about Assembly next day. I went into the kitchen and peeled

some potatoes for my mum. She was ever so
pleased when she came in from work and said I
must've known she'd brought me a present.

'Oh, thanks. What've you got me?'

She gave me a paper bag and when I opened it
I couldn't believe my eyes – a blooming
balaclava.

'There you are, now you won't be left out and
you can stop making my life a misery.'

'Thanks, Mum.'

If only my mum knew she was making *my* life a
misery. The balaclava she'd bought me was just
like the one I'd pinched. I felt sick. I didn't want
it. I couldn't wear it now. If I did, everybody

would say it was Norbert Lightowler's. Even if
they didn't, I just couldn't wear it. I wouldn't feel
it was mine. I had to get rid of it. I went outside
and put it down the lavatory. I had to pull the

chain three times before it went away. It's a good job we've got an outside lavatory or else my mum would have wondered what was wrong with me.

I could hardly eat my tea.

'What's wrong with you? Aren't you hungry?'

'No, not much.'

'What've you been eating? You've been eating sweets, haven't you?'

'No, I don't feel hungry.'

'Don't you feel well?'

'I'm all right.'

I wasn't, I felt terrible. I told my mum I was going upstairs to work on my model aeroplane.

'Well, it's my bingo night, so make yourself some cocoa before you go to bed.'

I went upstairs to bed, and after a while I fell asleep. The last thing I remember was a big balaclava, with a smiling face, and it was the Headmaster's face.

I was scared stiff when I went to school next morning. In Assembly it seemed different. All the boys were looking at me. Norbert Lightowler pushed past and didn't say anything. When prayers finished I just stood there waiting for the Headmaster to ask for the culprit to own up, but he was talking about the school fête. And then he said he had something very important to announce and I could feel myself going red. My ears were burning like anything and I was going hot and cold both at the same time.

33

'I'm very pleased to announce that the school football team has won the inter-league cup . . .'

And that was the end of Assembly, except that we were told to go and play in the schoolyard until we were called in, because there was a teachers' meeting. I couldn't understand why I hadn't been found out yet, but I still didn't feel any better, I'd probably be called to the Headmaster's room later on.

I went out into the yard. Everybody was happy because we were having extra playtime. I could see all the Balaclava Boys going round together. Then I saw Norbert Lightowler was one of them. I couldn't be sure it was Norbert because he had a balaclava on, so I had to go up close to him. Yes, it was Norbert. He must have bought a new balaclava that morning.

'Have you bought a new one then, Norbert?'

'Y'what?'

'You've bought a new balaclava, have you?'

'What are you talking about?'

'Your balaclava. You've got a new balaclava, haven't you?'

'No, I never lost it, at all. Some fool had shoved it down the sleeve of my raincoat.'

Fighting in Break

René Goscinny

'You're a liar,' I told Geoffrey.

'Say that again,' said Geoffrey.

'You're a liar,' I told him.

'Oh, I am, am I?' he asked me.

'Yes,' I said, 'you are,' and the bell went for the end of break.

'OK,' said Geoffrey, as we got in line, 'we have a fight at next break, right?'

'Right!' I said, because you don't catch me dodging a challenge! No fear!

'Silence there!' shouted Old Spuds who was on duty. It's best not to play him up.

Next lesson was geography. Alec, who was sitting beside me, said he'd hold my coat for me when I fought Geoffrey at break, and he advised me to hit him on the chin like boxers on the telly.

'No, you want to punch him on the nose!' said Eddie, who was sitting behind us. 'One good punch, wham! and you've won.'

'Wrong!' said Rufus, who was next to Eddie.

35

'Smack his face – that's what Geoffrey doesn't like.'

'Fool! How often have you seen boxers smacking each other's faces?' asked Max, who was sitting fairly close to us, and he passed a note to Jeremy who wanted to know what it was all about only from where he was sitting he couldn't hear.

Unfortunately, the note happened to reach Cuthbert and Cuthbert is teacher's pet and he put up his hand and said, 'Please, miss, I've got a note.'

Our teacher looked surprised and she asked Cuthbert to bring her the note, and Cuthbert went up to the front looking very pleased with himself.

Our teacher read the note, and she said, 'It seems that two of you are planning a fight during break. I don't know what about, and I don't want to know. But I warn you, I shall ask Mr Goodman after break, and the culprits will be severely punished. Alec, come up to the blackboard!'

So Alec got asked about the rivers of England, and he wasn't very good because the only ones he knew were the Thames which flows through London and the Avon where he went for his holidays last year. All our gang could hardly wait for next break; they were arguing like mad, and our teacher had to bang the table with her ruler and Matthew, who was asleep, thought it was meant for him and went to stand in the corner. I was worried, because if our teacher gave me detention there'd be trouble at home and I probably wouldn't get any of the chocolate mousse we were having for pudding. Or suppose our teacher had me expelled? That would be awful; Mum would be terribly sad and Dad would tell me how at my age he was an example to his little friends and what was the use of him bleeding himself white to give me a good education and I'd come to a bad end and it would be quite some time before I saw the inside of a cinema again. I had a big lump in my throat and the bell went for the end of the lesson, and I looked at Geoffrey and I realized he didn't seem to be in any hurry to go down to the playground either.

Out there, all the gang were waiting. 'Let's go to the far end of the playground,' said Max. 'We'll be private there.'

Geoffrey and I followed the others. Then Matthew turned round and said to Cuthbert, 'Not you! You told on them!'

'But I want to watch!' said Cuthbert, and then he said that if he couldn't watch he was going to go and tell Old Spuds this minute and no one would be able to fight and it jolly well served us right.

'Oh, let him watch!' said Rufus. 'After all, Geoffrey and Nicholas are going to get punished anyway, so it doesn't make any difference whether Cuthbert goes and tells on them before or afterwards.'

'We'll get punished,' said Geoffrey. 'We'll get punished if we fight, Nicholas. For the last time, do you take back what you said?'

'Don't be so daft! He isn't taking anything back!' said Alec.

'No fear!' said Max.

'Right, off you go,' said Eddie. 'I'll referee the fight.'

'You, be ref?' said Rufus. 'Don't make me laugh! Why should *you* be ref?'

'Don't let's quarrel over that!' said Jeremy. 'We'd better get a move on. Break will soon be over.'

' 'Scuse me,' said Geoffrey, 'but the ref is *most* important. I'm not fighting unless there's a good ref!'

'Hear, hear!' I said. 'Geoffrey's dead right.'

'OK, OK,' said Rufus. 'I'll be ref.'

Eddie didn't care for that, and he said Rufus didn't know the first thing about boxing, he even thought boxers smacked each other's faces.

'A smack from me is every bit as good as a punch on the nose from you!' said Rufus, and wham! he smacked Eddie's face. Eddie was furious, I've never seen him so furious before and he started fighting Rufus and he tried to punch his nose but Rufus wouldn't keep still and that made Eddie even angrier and he kept shouting that Rufus was a rotten sport.

'Stop it! Stop it!' yelled Alec. 'Break will soon be over.'

'Why don't you shut your big mouth, fatso?' asked Max.

So Alec asked me to hold his currant bun for him and he started fighting Max. I was really surprised at that, because Alec doesn't usually like fighting, specially not when he's eating a currant bun. The thing is that Alec's Mum made him take some kind of slimming pills, and ever since then he hasn't liked being called fatso. I was busy watching Alec and Max, so I don't know why Jeremy kicked Matthew, but I think it could have been because Matthew won a lot of marbles off Jeremy yesterday.

Anyway, all the gang were fighting like mad. It was terrific! I started eating Alec's currant bun and I gave a bit of it to Geoffrey. Then Old Spuds came hurrying up and he separated everyone, saying it was disgraceful and we'd see what we would see, and he went to ring the bell.

'There! What did I tell you?' said Alec. 'All this fooling about, and Geoffrey and Nicholas didn't even have time for their fight!'

When Old Spuds told her what had happened our teacher was very cross, and she gave the whole class detention except for Cuthbert and Geoffrey and me, and she said we were an example to the rest who were disgusting little savages.

'You were dead lucky the bell went!' said Geoffrey. 'I could hardly wait to start fighting you!'

'Don't make me laugh!' I said. 'Dirty liar!'

'Say that again!' said Geoffrey.

'Dirty liar!' I said. 'Right!' said Geoffrey. 'We'll have a fight next break.'

'OK,' I said.

Because, let me tell you, you don't catch me dodging a challenge. No fear!

Cheating

Susan Shreve

I cheated on a unit test in math class this morning during second period with Mr Burke. Afterward, I was too sick to eat lunch just thinking about it.

I came straight home from school, went to my room, and lay on the floor trying to decide whether it would be better to run away from home now or after supper. Mostly I wished I was dead.

It wasn't even an accident that I cheated.

Yesterday Mr Burke announced there'd be a unit test and anyone who didn't pass would have to come to school on Saturday, most particularly me, since I didn't pass the last unit test. He said that right out in front of everyone as usual. You can imagine how much I like Mr Burke.

But I did plan to study just to prove to him that I'm plenty smart – which I am mostly – except in math, which I'd be okay in if I'd memorize my times tables. Anyway, I got my desk ready to study on since it was stacked with about two million things. Just when I was ready to work, Nicho came into my room with our new rabbit and it jumped on my desk and knocked the flash cards all over the floor.

I yelled for my mother to come and help me pick them up, but Carlotta was crying as usual and Mother said I was old enough to help myself and a bunch of other stuff like that which mothers like to say. My mother's one of those people who tells you everything you've done wrong for thirty years like you do it every day. It drives me crazy.

Anyway, Nicho and I took the rabbit outside but then Philip came to my room and also Marty from next door and before long it was dinner. After dinner my father said I could watch a special on television if I'd done all my homework.

Of course I said I had.

That was the beginning. I felt terrible telling my father a lie about the homework so I couldn't even enjoy the special. I guessed he knew I was lying and was so disappointed he couldn't talk about it.

Not much is important in our family. Marty's mother wants him to look okay all the time and my friend Nathan has to do well in school and Andy has so many rules he must go crazy just trying to remember them. My parents don't bother making up a lot of rules. But we do have to tell the truth – even if it's bad, which it usually is. You can imagine how I didn't really enjoy the special.

It was nine o'clock when I got up to my room and that was too late to study for the unit test so I lay in my bed with the light off and decided what I would do the next day when I was in Mr B.'s math class not knowing the 8- and 9-times tables.

So, you see, the cheating was planned after all.

But at night, thinking about Mr B. – who could scare just about anybody I know, even my father – it seemed perfectly sensible to cheat. It didn't even seem bad when I thought of my parents' big thing about telling the truth.

I'd go into class jolly as usual, acting like things were going just great, and no one, not even Mr

B., would suspect the truth. I'd sit down next to Stanley Plummer – he is so smart in math it makes you sick – and from time to time, I'd glance over at his paper to copy the answers. It would be a cinch. In fact, every test before, I had to try hard not to see his answers because our desks are practically on top of each other.

And that's exactly what I did this morning. It was a cinch. Everything was okay except that my stomach was upside down and I wanted to die.

The fact is, I couldn't believe what I'd done in cold blood. I began to wonder about myself – really wonder – things like whether I would steal from stores or hurt someone on purpose or do some other terrible thing I couldn't even imagine. I began to wonder whether I was plain bad to the core.

I've never been a wonderful kid that everybody in the world loves and thinks is swell, like Nicho. I have a bad temper and I like to have my own way and I argue a lot. Sometimes I can be mean. But most of the time I've thought of myself as a pretty decent kid. Mostly I work hard, I stick up for little kids, and I tell the truth.Mostly I like myself fine – except I wish I were better at basketball.

Now all of a sudden I've turned into this criminal. It's hard to believe I'm just a boy. And all because of one stupid math test.

Lying on the floor of my room, I begin to think

that probably I've been bad all along. It just took this math test to clinch it. I'll probably never tell the truth again.

I tell my mother I'm sick when she calls me to come down for dinner. She doesn't believe me, but puts me to bed anyhow. I lie there in the early winter darkness wondering what terrible thing I'll be doing next when my father comes in and sits down on my bed.

'What's the matter?' he asks.

'I've got a stomach ache,' I say. Luckily, it's too dark to see his face.

'Is that all?'

'Yeah.'

'Mommy says you've been in your room since school.'

'I was sick there, too,' I say.

'She thinks something happened today and you're upset.'

That's the thing that really drives me crazy about my mother. She knows things sitting inside my head same as if I was turned inside out.

'Well,' my father says. I can tell he doesn't believe me.

'My stomach *is* feeling sort of upset,' I hedge.

'Okay,' he says and he pats my leg and gets up.

Just as he shuts the door to my room I call out to him in a voice I don't even recognize as my

45

own that I'm going to have to run away.

'How come?' he calls back, not surprised or anything.

So I tell him I cheated on this math test. To tell the truth, I'm pretty much surprised at myself. I didn't plan to tell him anything.

He doesn't say anything at first and that just about kills me. I'd be fine if he'd spank me or something. To say nothing can drive a person crazy.

And then he says I'll have to call Mr Burke.

It's not what *I* had in mind.

'Now?' I ask, surprised.

'Now,' he says. He turns on the light and pulls off my covers.

'I'm not going to,' I say.

But I do it. I call Mr Burke, probably waking him up, and I tell him exactly what happened, even that I decided to cheat the night before the test. He says I'll come in Saturday to take another test, which is okay with me, and I thank him a whole lot for being understanding and all. He's not friendly but he's not absolutely mean either.

'Today I thought I was turning into a criminal,' I tell my father when he turns out my light.

Sometimes my father kisses me good night and sometimes he doesn't. I never know. But tonight he does.

Mrs Pepperpot to the Rescue

Alf Prøysen

When it is breaking-up day at the village school, and the summer holidays are about to begin, all the children bring flowers to decorate the school. They pick them in their own gardens or get them from their uncles and aunts, and then they carry their big bunches along the road, while they sing and shout because it is the end of term. Their mothers and fathers wave to them from the windows and wish them a happy breaking-up day.

But in one window stands a little old woman who just watches the children go by. That is Mrs Pepperpot.

She has no one now to wish a happy breaking-up day, for all her own children are long since grown up and gone away, and none of the young ones think of asking her for flowers.

At least, that is not quite true; I do know of one little girl who picked flowers in Mrs Pepperpot's garden. But that was several years ago, not long after the little old woman first started shrinking

to the size of a pepperpot at the most incon-
venient moments.

That particular summer Mrs Pepperpot's garden was fairly bursting with flowers: there were
white lilac with boughs almost laden to the
ground, blue and red anemones on strong,
straight stalks, poppies with graceful nodding
yellow heads and many other lovely flowers. But
no one had asked Mrs Pepperpot for any of
them, so she just stood in her window and
watched as the children went by, singing and
shouting, on their way to the breaking-up day at
school.

The very last to cross the yard in front of her
house was a little girl, and she was walking, oh,
so slowly, and carried nothing in her hands. Mrs
Pepperpot's cat was lying on the doorstep and
greeted her with a 'Miaow!' But the little girl only
made a face and said, 'Stupid animal!' And when
Mrs Pepperpot's dog, which was chained to the
wall, started barking and wagging his tail the
little girl snapped, 'Hold your tongue!'

Then Mrs Pepperpot opened the window to
throw a bone out to the dog and the little girl
whirled round and shouted angrily, 'Don't throw
that dirty bone on my dress!'

That was enough. Mrs Pepperpot put her
hands on her hips and told the little girl that no
one had any right to cross the yard in front of her
house and throw insulting words at her or her cat

and dog, which were doing no harm to anybody.

The little girl began to cry. 'I want to go home,' she sobbed. 'I've an awful pain in my tummy and I don't want to go to the breaking-up party! Why should I go when I have a pain in my tummy?'

'Where's your mother, child?' asked Mrs Pepperpot.

'None of your business!' snapped the girl.

'Well, where's your father, then?' asked Mrs Pepperpot.

'Never you mind!' said the girl, still more rudely. 'But if you want to know why I don't want to go to school today it's because I haven't any flowers. We haven't a garden, anyway, as we've only been here since Christmas. But Dad's going to build us a house now that he's working at the ironworks, and then we'll have a garden. My mum makes paper flowers and does the paper round, see? Anything more you'd like to know? Oh well, I might as well go to school, I suppose. Teacher can say what she likes – I don't care! If *she'd* been going from school to school for three years she wouldn't know much either! So blow her and her flowers!' And the little girl stared defiantly at Mrs Pepperpot.

Mrs Pepperpot stared back at the little girl and then she said: 'That's the spirit! But I think I can help you with the flowers. Just you go out in the garden and pick some lilac and anemones and poppies and anything else you like. I'll go and find some paper for you to wrap them in.'

So the girl went into the garden and started picking flowers while Mrs Pepperpot went indoors for some paper. But just as she was coming back to the door she shrank!

Roly Poly! And there she was, tucked up in the paper like jam in a pudding, when the little girl came running back with her arms full of flowers.

'Here we are!' shouted the little girl.

'And here *we* are!' said Mrs Pepperpot as she disentangled herself from the paper. 'Don't be scared; this is something that happens to me from time to time, and I never know when I'm going to shrink. But now I've got an idea; I want you to pop me in your satchel and take me along with you to school. We're going to have a game with them all! What's your name, by the way?'

'It's Rita,' said the little girl who was staring at Mrs Pepperpot with open mouth.

'Well, Rita, don't just stand there. Hurry up and put the paper round those flowers. There's no time to lose!'

When they got to the school the breaking-up party was well under way, and the teacher didn't look particularly pleased even when Rita handed her the lovely bunch of flowers. She just nodded and said, 'Thanks.'

'Take no notice,' said Mrs Pepperpot from Rita's satchel.

'Go to your desk,' said the teacher. Rita sat

down with her satchel on her knee.

'We'll start with a little arithmetic,' said the teacher. 'What are seven times seven?'

'Forty-nine!' whispered Mrs Pepperpot from the satchel.

'Forty-nine!' said Rita.

This made the whole class turn round and stare at Rita, for up to now she had hardly been able to count to thirty! But Rita stared back at them and smiled. Then she stole a quick look at her satchel.

'What's that on your lap?' asked the teacher. 'Nobody is allowed to use a crib. Give me your satchel at once!'

So Rita had to carry it up to the teacher's desk where it was hung on a peg.

The teacher went on to the next question: 'If we take fifteen from eighteen what do we get?'

All the children started counting on their fingers, but Rita saw that Mrs Pepperpot was sticking both her arms and one leg out of the satchel.

'Three!' said Rita before the others had had time to answer.

This time nobody suspected her of cheating and Rita beamed all over while Mrs Pepperpot waved to her from between the pages of her exercise book.

'Very strange, I must say,' said the teacher. 'Now we'll have a little history and geography.

Which country is it that has a long wall running round it and has the oldest culture in the world?'

Rita was watching the satchel the whole time, and now she saw Mrs Pepperpot's head pop up again. The little old woman had smeared her face with yellow chalk and now she put her fingers in the corners of her eyes and pulled them into narrow slits.

'China!' shouted Rita.

The teacher was quite amazed at this answer, but she had to admit that Rita was right. Then she made an announcement.

'Children,' she said, 'I have decided to award a treat to the one of you who gave the most right answers. Rita gave me all the right answers, so she is the winner, and she will be allowed to serve coffee to the teachers in the staff-room afterwards.'

Rita felt very pleased and proud; she was so used to getting meals ready when she was alone at home that she was sure she could manage this all right. So, when the other children went home, she took her satchel from the teacher's desk and went out into the kitchen. But, oh dear, it wasn't a bit like home! The coffee-pot was far too big and the huge cake with icing on it was very different from the plate of bread-and-dripping she usually got ready for her parents at home. Luckily the cups and saucers and plates and spoons had all been laid out on the table beforehand. All the same, it seemed too much to Rita and she just sat down and cried. In a moment she heard the sound of scratching from the satchel, and out stepped Mrs Pepperpot.

'If you're the girl I take you for,' said the little old woman, putting her hands on her hips, 'you won't give up half-way like this! Come on, just you lift me up on the table, we'll soon have this job done! As far as I could see from my hiding place, there are nine visiting teachers and your own Miss Snooty. That makes two cups of water and two dessertspoons of coffee per person – which makes twenty cups of water and twenty dessertspoons of coffee in all – right?'

'I think so. Oh, you're wonderful!' said Rita, drying her tears. 'I'll measure out the water and coffee at once, but I don't know how I'm going to cut up that cake!'

'That'll be all right,' said Mrs Pepperpot. 'As far as I can see the cake is about ninety paces – my paces – round. So if we divide it by ten that'll make each piece nine paces. But that will be too big for each slice, so we'll divide nine by three and make each piece three paces thick. Right?'

'I expect so,' said Rita, who was getting a bit lost.

'But first we must mark a circle in the middle of the cake,' went on Mrs Pepperpot. 'Lift me up on your hand, please.'

Rita lifted her carefully on to her hand.

'Now take me by the legs and turn me upside down. Then, while you swing me round, I can mark a circle with one finger in the icing. Right; let's go!'

So Rita swung Mrs Pepperpot round upside down and the result was a perfect little circle drawn right in the middle of the cake.

'Crumbs are better than no bread!' said Mrs Pepperpot as she stood there, swaying giddily and licking her finger. 'Now I'll walk right round the cake, and at every third step I want you to make a little notch in the icing with the knife. Here we go!

> *'One, two, three, notch!*
> *One, two, three, notch!*
> *One, two, three, notch!'*

And in this way Mrs Pepperpot marched all round the cake, and Rita notched it so that it made exactly thirty slices when it was cut.

When they had finished someone called from the staff-room: 'Where's that clever girl with the coffee? Hurry up and bring it in, dear, then you can fetch the cake afterwards.' Rita snatched up the big coffee-pot, which was boiling now and hurried in with it, and Mrs Pepperpot stood listening to the way the teachers praised Rita as she poured the coffee into the cups with a steady hand.

After a while she came out for the cake. Mrs Pepperpot clapped her hands: 'Well done, Rita! There's nothing to worry about now.'

But she shouldn't have said that, for while she was listening to the teachers telling Rita again how clever she was, she suddenly heard that Miss Snooty raising her voice:

'I'm afraid you've forgotten two things, dear,' she said.

'Oh dear!' thought Mrs Pepperpot, 'the cream-jug and the sugar-bowl! I shall have to look and see if they are both filled.'

The cream-jug was full, but when Mrs Pepperpot leaned over the edge of the sugar-bowl she toppled in! And at the same moment Rita rushed in, put the lid on the sugar-bowl and put it and the cream-jug on a little tray. Then she turned round and went back to the staff-room.

First Mrs Pepperpot wondered if she should tell Rita where she was, but she was afraid the child might drop the tray altogether, so instead she buried herself well down in the sugar-bowl and hoped for the best.

Rita started carrying the tray round. But her teacher hadn't finished with her yet. 'I hope you remembered the sugar-tongs,' she said.

Rita didn't know what to say, but Mrs Pepperpot heard the remark, and when the visiting head teacher took the lid off, Mrs Pepperpot popped up like a jack-in-the-box holding a lump of sugar in her outstretched hand. She stared straight in front of her and never moved an eyelid, so the head teacher didn't notice anything odd. He simply took the sugar lump and waved Rita on with the tray. But his neighbour at the table looked hard at Mrs Pepperpot and said: 'What very curious sugar-tongs – I suppose they're made of plastic. Whatever will they think of next?' Then he asked Rita if she had brought them with her from home, and she said yes, which was strictly true of course.

After that everyone wanted to have a look at the curious sugar-tongs, till in the end Rita's teacher called her over.

'Let me have a look at those tongs,' she said. She reached out her hand to pick them up, but this was too much for Mrs Pepperpot. In a moment she had the whole tray over and everything fell on the floor. The cream jug was smashed and the contents of the sugar-bowl rolled under the cupboard, which was just as well for Mrs Pepperpot!

But the teacher thought it was she who had upset the tray, and suddenly she was sorry she had been so hard on the little girl. She put her arms round Rita and gave her a hug. 'It was all my fault,' she said. 'You've been a very good little parlourmaid.'

Later, when all the guests had gone, and Rita was clearing the table, the teacher pointed to the dark corner by the cupboard and said, 'Who is that standing there?'

And out stepped Mrs Pepperpot as large as life and quite unruffled. 'I've been sent to lend a hand with the washing-up,' she said. 'Give me that tray, Rita. You and I will go out into the kitchen.'

When at last the two of them were walking home, Rita said, 'Why did you help me all day when I was so horrid to you this morning?'

'Well,' said Mrs Pepperpot, 'perhaps it was because you *were* so horrid. Next time maybe I'll help that Miss Snooty of yours. She looks pretty horrid too, but she might be nice underneath.'

One Good Turn
Lilith Norman

They were walking home, Joanne, her mother
and her friend Patricia. Joanne was miles away,
day-dreaming about the film they had just seen.

'Quick, Joanne, run and open the gate for that
lady.'

Joanne looked up with a start. A tall woman,
with an armload of flowers, was struggling to
undo the latch of a gate. She was the most beautiful woman Joanne had ever seen.

But before Joanne could move, Patricia darted forward. The gate swung open and the woman went through. Patricia waited till she was inside and shut the gate again. The woman gave Patricia a dazzling smile. 'Thank you *so* much,' she said.

Joanne felt hot inside. That smile and that thank-you should have been hers. Mum had asked her to open the gate, not Patricia. What made it even worse was Patricia's smug look as she bounced back to Joanne and her mother.

Before she knew what she was doing, Joanne's hand clenched, and her fist came up. *Thunk*! It landed on the side of Patricia's head. Patricia's mouth dropped open and her eyes filled with tears. Joanne stared at her, hard-eyed. Patricia turned and ran; away up the street and in at her own gate.

'Joanne!' Mrs Ballard grabbed Joanne's arm. 'What on earth – ? How dare you do that!'

Joanne said nothing.

Mrs Ballard looked at her daughter's hot face and tight lips. She shook her head, but she didn't say anything more. They walked home in silence.

Before Joanne went to sleep that night, her mother came into her room. 'You must apologize to Patricia first thing tomorrow morning,' she said. 'I've already spoken to her mother and said how sorry *I* am. It was a dreadful thing to do to your best friend – and for no reason at all.'

Joanne looked dumbly at her mother. There was a reason – if a smile and a thank-you could be a reason. 'I'm not sorry,' she said sulkily.

'I don't care if you're sorry or not,' said Mrs Ballard. 'You're still going to apologize. I won't have you running around acting like a little hooligan.'

'All right,' mumbled Joanne. She turned over and stared out the window. When her mother leant over to kiss her goodnight she hunched her back away.

Next morning Joanne got to school later than usual. She would have to apologize – Mum was sure to find out if she didn't. Not that it mattered much now. It was all over; it had happened yesterday. Probably Patricia would have forgotten about it by now.

Joanne hoped so. The thought of saying she was sorry made her feel hot all over. It was so hard to *say* it, to make the words come out. And who would she play with all day or talk to? Without Patricia she felt loose and rattly, like a marble in a bucket.

She looked around the playground. Patricia was down near the bubblers. Gwenda and Helen and Susie were with her. They were all looking at Patricia's head. Joanne walked slowly towards them.

She heard Helen say, 'What an awful bruise.'

Joanne sidled closer. All she could see was the tiniest lump.

'You can play with us today,' Susie said, and slipped her arm under Patricia's.

'Oh yes,' said Gwenda. She saw Joanne coming closer, and raised her voice. 'We don't like nasty tough girls who hit people,' she added. She pursed her lips primly, then smirked at Joanne.

Patricia turned round to see what Gwenda was looking at. Gwenda and Helen and Susie drew together, making a smug little wall behind Patricia.

Joanne opened her mouth to speak, but the words wouldn't come. Patricia took two steps towards her and – *thunk*!

Joanne's head rang.

Gwenda and Helen and Susie twittered in horror. 'Ooh! She *hit* her!' 'Patricia hit Joanne!' 'Bully!' They turned and ran down to a safer part of the school yard, where there were no nasty, rough girls.

Joanne bit her lip. She wouldn't cry. Instead she said, 'Mum said I had to say I was sorry. Now I don't have to.'

Patricia looked disappointed for a moment. Then she shrugged. 'No, I suppose we're even now. Fair's fair.'

They stood looking at one another. Then they both began to giggle.

'I've got chocolate crackles for play lunch,' said

Patricia. 'I'll swap you one.'

'Okay,' said Joanne. 'You can have half of my apple.' She rubbed her head hard. With a bit of luck they'd soon have matching bruises.

The School

Richard Hughes

Once there was a schoolmaster and a schoolmistress who hadn't any school.

'This is absurd,' they said. 'We *must* have a
school': so they got a brass plate, and wrote the
word 'SCHOOL' on it, and put it up on their gate.

The next day they rang a bell at nine o'clock in
the morning for lessons to begin. But of course
no one came. So for half the morning he taught
her, and for the other half she taught him.

The next day he said, 'I am going out to see if I
can't find someone to come to our school.' On
the way he passed a toy shop, and in the window
there was a fine big Noah's Ark; so he bought it
and took it home. Then he took out Mr and Mrs
Noah, and Shem and Ham and Japhet and all the
animals and put them in the desks in the
schoolroom.

'Now,' he said, 'we have got a splendid big
class to teach!'

So all that day they taught the things out of

the Ark.

'I do think this is a well-behaved class,' said the schoolmistress. 'They sit ever so still and never make any noise at all!'

Which was perfectly true. They never made a sound. The only trouble was that when you asked them a question they still didn't make a sound, but just sat quiet and didn't answer.

'What do two and two make, Noah?' the schoolmistress asked.

But Mr Noah said nothing.

'Next!' she said.

But Mrs Noah said nothing either.

'Next! Next! Next!' said she. But Shem and Ham and Japhet and the two lions and the two elephants and the two mice and all the other animals said nothing either.

'What *I* think,' said the schoolmistress, 'is that we've got the stupidest class that ever was!'

So she popped them all back in the Ark and went out to look for something else.

Presently she came to a shop called 'Railway Umbrellas'. It was where they sell all the things people leave in railway carriages and never come back for: umbrellas, and handbags, and bananas, and babies, and concertinas, and parcels, and so on. So she went in. And sitting in the window she saw a dear little black kitten.

'Is that a railway kitten too?' she asked the man.

'Yes, madam,' he said. 'Somebody left him in a basket on the rack of a train only the other day.'

'Well, I'll have that one then,' she said, and bought it and took it home. When lesson time came they took all the creatures out of the Ark and made the kitten sit in the middle of them.

'What do two and two make, Railway Kitten?' she asked.

'Meaow!' said the kitten.

'No, they don't, they make four!' she said. 'What is the capital of Italy?'

'Meaow!' said the kitten.

'Wrong! It's Rome. Who signed Magna Charta?'

'Meaow!' said the Railway Kitten.

'Wrong again,' she said, 'it was King John! I've never even heard of Mr Meaow!' And she turned round and started to write a sum on the blackboard. But as soon as her back was turned the naughty Railway Kitten began to have a lovely game with all the wooden creatures out of the Ark. He knocked them down, and sent them skidding all over the floor: and when the schoolmistress looked round again he had climbed on his desk, dipped his tail in the inkpot and now was swishing it about so as to flip ink all over the room.

'Oh, you *naughty* kitten!' she cried. 'If you're not good I'll send you back to your railway!' And she took him and shut him up in the kitchen.

Just then the front-door bell rang and the schoolmaster went to see who it was. Outside there was a little girl, with a packet of school books under her arm.

'Please,' she said, 'I've forgotten the way to my school; may I come to yours instead?'

'Certainly! Certainly!' said the schoolmaster. So she came in, and hung her hat and coat on a peg and changed her shoes, and went and sat down in the schoolroom.

Now, not only was she as good as the Ark creatures, and sat perfectly still and quiet, but also when she was asked a question she answered it, and always got the answer right. And she never once let the Railway Kitten play during lessons, though out of lesson time of course she played with him a lot, and gave him his saucer of milk.

When the evening came she said: 'Is this a boarding school? Because if it is I don't think I shall bother to go home.'

'All right,' they said and put her to bed.

Now, as I have told you, all day she had been good as good: but when she went to bed there was just one thing she was naughty about: she WOULD NOT get out of the bath when she was told. When she had been washed she just lay back and refused to move, and the poor school-mistress simply *couldn't* make her. She lay there till the hot water turned her as pink as a lobster, and it wasn't till the water had got quite cold that she would come out. Then, of course, she was cold too, and shivered, and her teeth chattered when she got into bed.

The next day she was perfectly good again: but when night came the same thing happened – once she was in her bath she *would not* move.

'I am going to count one – two – three and then pull up the plug!' said the schoolmistress. 'ONE – ! TWO – ! – '

And before she could say THREE the little girl jumped out in a terrible fright.

'That's a good plan,' thought the schoolmistress, 'I'll do it again.'

And so she did. Every night, when the little girl wouldn't get out, she counted ONE, TWO, and before she could say THREE out she jumped. And this went on for a whole week. But when it came to a Saturday night, and she counted ONE! TWO! all the little girl said was 'SHAN'T!' and lay so flat on the bottom of the bath that only her nose was above the water.

'THREE!' said the mistress, and pulled up the plug! Away the water rushed, down the waste pipe, and alas! away went the poor little girl with it. First her feet were sucked into the hole, and then her legs, and then her body, and in a moment she had disappeared altogether.

'OH, what *have* you done,' cried the schoolmaster. 'You have lost our only child!'

'I don't care!' said the schoolmistress in a stern voice.

'She should have got out of the bath when she was told!'

The Egg-Shaped Boy

June Counsel

Nobody liked Ovey very much. He was an egg-shaped boy. His head was large, his shoulders sloped, his arms were short, so were his legs, and his tum was fat. He couldn't run, couldn't throw, couldn't catch, or not as 3R understood running and throwing and catching, not as Jake Todd understood them. 'He's hopeless,' scowled Jake, who was ace at all three. Ovey laughed at jokes no one else could see. 'He's batty,' shrugged brilliant Dawn Fairley, who was mad on science and liked to see things plainly. Ovey never listened. His desk was right under Mr Rules but it might have been in China for all the notice he took.

'Now then, class, do you understand?' Mr Rules would ask. 'Have I made it clear? Ovey, what have I just been saying?'

'H'mm?' Ovey would say, gazing at Mr Rules as though he had just materialized from outer space, and he wouldn't have heard a word.

'He's thick,' Mr Rules told the staffroom, despairingly.

Ovey hadn't been long at St Jude's, but long enough to know he didn't fit.

'Now in a book,' said Ovey, talking to himself as he plodded through the rain, 'I would meet a wizard and rescue him from difficulty and he would grant me a wish and I would wish to be . . .'

He sloshed a great wave forward from a puddle and trod heavily on to a foot coming towards him.

'To be what?' asked a crackling voice above his head.

'Popular,' finished Ovey, hitting his nose

against the third button of a dark green raincoat.

A sneeze exploded above him. Strong fingers clutched his shoulder.

'Are you by any miracle going to St Jude the Obscure?' asked the voice, creaking like an old door.

'I'm going to St Jude's the Poor,' replied Ovey, looking up. Through his rain-blurred glasses he saw a white beard, a Roman nose, bristling white eyebrows. Rain dripped from these sharp features on to his own pudgy ones.

'I beg you, take me there,' said the man. 'I can *not* find the way in and if I'm not there soon I'm going back to bed.'

'People always get lost the first time they try to find St Jude's,' Ovey told him. 'I often go past the entrance myself, sometimes for quite a long way.'

'Then let us leave this puddle, friendly though it is,'croaked the man, 'and, as we go, tell me why you want to be popular.'

'Because,' began Ovey as they set off, 'I haven't any friends. I'm not interested in the things the others like to do, and they're not interested in the things I like to do, so we bore each other.'

'Do they tease you?'

'A bit.' This was a cover-up. 3R teased Ovey a lot, sometimes kindly, sometimes cruelly, depending on how bored they were. 'They draw egg shapes and turn them into me. I call them morons and they call me useless, but it would be nice,' cried Ovey, finishing on a strong thought, 'if I had just one thing that they wanted and only I could give them.'

They turned this way and that and came to St Jude's the Poor County Junior School, looking poorly indeed in the pouring rain.

'Cor, look at that puddle!' cried Ovey. 'What a whopper!'

'We're very late,' said the man. 'They've all gone in. What will happen to you?'

'I'm usually late,' said Ovey, 'because I don't like coming much. I get late marks all the time. I'll take you to the Secretary's office.'

The Secretary came gushing out. 'Oh, Mr Venables, we are relieved to see you. We thought you'd got lost.'

The Head popped up as if by magic. 'Good gracious, Mr Venables, have you *walked*? Let me take your coat.'

Mr Rules shot forward rubbing his hands. *Sir* here, wondered Ovey, why isn't he in the classroom?

'I'm jolly glad you got here, Mr Venables, my class would have been disappointed if you hadn't come. Let me get you a cup of coffee. White? With sugar?'

'Black, please, without,' said Venables, for clearly that was the stranger's name, 'thank you.'

He stretched out a long arm and twirled Ovey round just as Ovey was slipping off.

'Bear witness, lords, and lady, you owe my presence to this squire of low degree. He rescued me from a maze of mean streets and brought me here –' he broke off to sneeze violently.

'Well, it seems your lateness has paid off for once, Ovey,' said Mr Rules. 'Cut along now and tell 3R that Mr Venables is here and that I'll be bringing him up as soon as he's dry and warm.'

So the whitebearded man was expected and coming to see 3R, but who on earth is he, wondered Ovey. Well, Venables of course, but who is Venables?

'Mr Venables has come and Sir's bringing him up presently,' said Ovey as soon as he got into the classroom. 'Who is he?'

3R who had broken into a cheer, stopped and stared at him in wonder.

'It's unbelievable,' said Wilkes the class genius, 'just unbelievable. All *week*, practically all *term*, we've been reading Vernon Venables' books. Sir only finished reading the last one yesterday.'

'What book?' asked Ovey bewildered.

' "The Case of the Cracked Pot" ' bawled 3R furiously.

'Oh, that,' said Ovey. 'I didn't listen. It bored me.'

Into the astounded silence that followed this remark, walked first Mr Rules, then Mr Venables, divested of his hat and raincoat and wearing a Norfolk jacket, which is a jacket famous for pockets.

'Well now, 3R, a big welcome for Mr Vernon Venables who has actually come here on *foot* to speak to us, and on a day like this! What do you think of that? Mr Venables, we finished your book "The Case of the Cracked Pot" yesterday,' Venables pulled a face, 'and I know 3R will want to ask you where you get such super ideas from. Unfortunately 'flu has struck down one of our teachers and I have to go and look after her class, but I know you are going to have a one hundred per cent attentive' – here his eye fell upon Ovey gazing dreamily out of the window – 'well, a – a ninety-nine per cent attentive audience. Wilkes here, who's a great fan of yours,' Wilkes stood up, proud and beaming, 'will bring you down to the staffroom when the bell goes, so I leave you in good hands.'

'Thank you,' said Venables, 'but I already have a squire.' He gestured at Ovey, who turned round at the sound of his voice. 'He will be my right-hand man.'

'Oh! Well, if you say so,' said Mr Rules doubtfully, 'though I should warn you that as a right hand, Ovey is usually two left feet. Sit down then, Wilkes. Thank you, Mr Venables.'

He smiled and went out. Venables regarded 3R morosely.

'So you are the Three Rs? Squire, bring me a glass of water, please.'

He swallowed painfully and pulled a soupmix packet from his righthand pocket and put it on the table in front of him. Then he pulled a Dream Swirl packet from his lefthand pocket and put that down. Then he put his hand in the top righthand pocket and brought out a clutch of tea and coffee bags and threw them down, then from his left top pocket some soup and stock cubes. Then he put his left hand into all his pockets and brought out more packets, and then he did it all again, and again, and again, till the table before him was piled high with a shining mountain of brightly coloured packets.

'Who's your best catcher? Who never misses a thing?'

'Me, me, me,' chorused 3R and hands shot up like fireworks.

'Ha!' said Venables and began whizzing the packets with skill, speed and trickery, some high, some low, some fast, some slow, some far, some near, some here, some there. The air was thick with flying missiles, waving hands, shrieks of glee or gasps of woe. Chairs overturned, heads bumped against heads, bodies scrabbled on the floor. Through the mêlée came Ovey, steadfastly guarding a beaker of water he was carrying from the sink. He put it down on the table, empty now save for one battered box of soup cubes.

'Thank you,' smiled Venables. He picked up the box of soup cubes. 'All that's left, I'm afraid.' And threw it to Ovey, who dropped it.

'Right now. Heads up. Bottoms on chairs. Now, what have all these things got in common? You, lad.' He pointed at Jake.

Jake frowned, stared, stared at his neighbours, cogitated, and read glumly, 'Soup in a Second. Just add water.'

'And you, fan of mine, Wilkes, is it? What does yours say?'

'Make that Stew Stupendous! Empty contents into saucepan, measure in half a litre of cold water and bring gently to the boil, stirring all the time,' read Wilkes rapidly.

'And yours?' Venables asked, lifting his white eyebrows at the Dodgy Boys' table.

The Dodgy Boys studied the picture on their packet. 'Pour on boiling water?' they guessed.

'Right,' said Venables, 'and yours?' turning to Dawn, but she frowned and answered, 'I haven't finished yet.' She was comparing the list of ingredients on all the packets and writing down the commonest ones.

'I've got it,' cried Ovey suddenly, 'they're all instant!'

'Right, squire, they are. Now, we're going to . . .'

'Please, sir,' interrupted Jake, 'aren't you going to talk about "The Case of the Cracked Pot"?'

'No, I am not,' rasped Venables, 'that book bores me. I laboured to write it and it reads laboriously. We're going to make our *own* story and we're starting right here with an ordinary everyday commonplace thing like a packet of processed food from the supermarket. So, come on, the Three Rs, let's be having you. Stir your brains.'

3R groaned and scratched, turning the packets this way and that. The Dodgy Boys began throwing theirs about. Ovey, who had begun to take the soup cubes out of the box, let out a shout.

'This one's different! It's not a soup cube at all. It's – it's,' he rushed to the science table and got the magnifying glass, 'roundish and lumpy and goes up to a point. The point's white, then it goes dark green, then light green, then there's a white line all round it, then it's blue.'

'What's it say?' screamed 3R.

'It's weeny writing,' grumbled Ovey, peering, 'it says – it says "Instant Island. Drop into deep water." '

Instantly 3R brightened like flowers after rain. The Dodgy Boys stopped throwing their packets about and Wilkes felt a hundred brilliant ideas flood his brain.

'There's a terrific puddle in the playground,' cried Ovey, excitedly, 'let's drop it in there.'

A howl of laughter went up. 'It's not real, dumbo, Mr Venables made it.'

'We can't go out in this rain,' sneered Jake. 'Sir wouldn't allow it.'

'We can,' Ovey insisted. 'We can put our anoraks on. It won't take a minute if it's instant. We can, can't we, sir?' He looked at Venables, who had shrunk down into his chair.

'You can do anything, in a story, provided you make people believe it,' whispered Venables, whose voice seemed to have disappeared. 'They must forget they're listening and *feel* they're *there*.'

With an effort he got up and put his hands on Ovey's shoulders.

'My voice won't carry 3R to the island. You must take them for me, squire.' He turned Ovey to face the class who were getting restless, and said, forcing his voice to reach them, 'You don't have to go into the yard and get wet to reach the island. You have to do a much harder thing. You have to listen.'

He pulled a shining steel pen from his pocket and folded Ovey's fingers round it. 'I hand the tale to Ovey. If he can transport you all to the Instant Island without one of you leaving the classroom, this pen is his. Help him to win it.'

3R gasped. Venables sat down. Ovey raised his hands like a conductor and began,

'Ovey dashed out followed by . . .'

'You're talking about yourself,' cried several voices.

'I'm in the story,' replied Ovey swiftly. 'You'll be in, if you listen.'

3R shut up like clams, and listened.

Ovey dashed out, followed by the Dodgy Boys, who would always sooner be wet and splashing than dry and working, and Dawn ('It'll be an experiment') and Wilkes ('It'll be a laugh') and Jake.

Of course nothing happened. How could it? The rain struck the surface of the puddle with such force that it made little fountains like white shuttlecocks. Long after Ovey had unwrapped the dry little lump and thrown it in, he and the others went on staring at the puddle, partly because it is difficult to stop staring at rain falling on puddles (or at water doing anything) and partly because it made them feel so dreamy and contented. Seconds and minutes and minutes passed and still they stared and it wasn't until the dark green humps and bumps below the white point had come up, that Dawn spoke.

'That's the mountain peak with snow on it, and below it's tropical rainforest. The dark folds are valleys. We'll see the rivers when the light green comes up . . .'

It was a super island. The rain seemed to withdraw from around it, though they could still hear the hiss of it falling at the back of them.

'Come on, beach,' urged Wilkes. 'I want to get

there.'

The beach came, blindingly white. The sea was blue and the Dodgy Boys saw to their joy that there were sharks.

Jake flung off his winter clobber and dived into turquoise water that felt like warm silk. Dawn made her anorak into a sock and began picking up shell after shell after shell, each one different, working her way towards the reef which kept the sharks out of the lagoon. Wilkes spun round and round in a delirium of excitement.

'So much stimuli!' he cried. 'What shall I do first? Write a poem, paint a picture, carve a coconut, make a raft, build a hut?'

The Dodgy Boys vanished into the jungle, from which, presently, came a wild squawking of parrots and chattering of monkeys as they made their riotous way inland. Ovey stood pondering. I shall climb the mountain, he thought. I want to stand on that peak.

It was a hard climb, but he made it. After the glare of the beach, the steam of the jungle, the silent snow was bliss. The air was so clear he could see Jake swimming in the lagoon, Dawn treading delicately over the reef, Wilkes walking up and down the beach with an enormous palm leaf on his head, looking like the letter T. In a clearing in the jungle, he saw the Dodgy Boys each with a parrot, teaching it to swear.

'It's idyllic,' breathed Ovey, and as he said this

a cloud of black ink darkened the water beneath Jake. He gave a single cry and disappeared. Far out on the reef, Dawn heard the cry and went racing towards it, a razor-sharp shell in her hand.

Ovey hurled himself down the mountain, forgetting that any rash movement might start an avalanche. Halfway down on a projecting rock that overhung the jungle, he saw a sight that redoubled his haste, a line of painted warriors stealing through the trees towards the Dodgy Boys. They had stone axes in their hands and from their belts dangled shrivelled brown objects that bobbed and bounced.

'Headhunters!' gasped Ovey. He came to a waterfall and went leaping down it from rock to rock, his brain hammering. Could Jake hold out till Dawn got there? Would the parrots warn the Dodgy Boys of the headhunters' approach? What would happen when Wilkes put his foot in that hole that had suddenly appeared in the sand?

Mr Rules, panting up the corridor, pushed open the door of 3R and heard Ovey's voice, strong, resonant, excited, carrying utter conviction.

'. . . what *was* coming out of the hole over which Wilkes's foot was poised? A wide, wicked mouth crowned with teeth that gleamed like daggers!'

For an impossible moment, as he listened, Mr Rules heard the boom of surf beating on a coral reef, felt the heat of a tropical sun, heard dis-

tinctly the squawking of parrots. Then he shook
his head and walked in. The scene was so extraordinary that he thought in panic, I'm hal-
lucinating, I've caught the 'flu. For Ovey, *Ovey*,
was standing up in front of the whole class talking and waving his hands, and every head was
turned to him. Even the awful Dodge twins and
their terrible cousin, William Dodge, were
listening. They look quite normal when they're
listening, thought Mr Rules dazedly. He saw that
Ovey clutched a steel pen in his right hand. Then
he saw Venables, sitting on a chair against the
wall, flushed and shivering, and he also was
listening to Ovey.

Venables rose and came over to Mr Rules
behind Ovey. Pointing to his throat, he
mouthed, 'Voice went. Ovey took over.'

Alarmed, Mr Rules looked at him. 'Mr Venables, you're ill. You've got this beastly 'flu. I'll
run you home at once.'

The dinner bell clanged. 'Go on, Ovey, go on,
don't stop,' pleaded the whole of 3R in anguish.

Mr Rules slipped his hand under Mr Venables'
elbow and felt him shaking with fever. 'Right,
3R,' he called, 'Mr Venables isn't well so I'm
taking him home now. We'll write him a thank
you letter this afternoon to tell him how much
we've enjoyed his visit. Home boys, go home.
Dinner boys, go to dinner, and likewise girls.
Well done, Ovey, you saved the day. You can

finish the story after dinner.' 3R cheered wildly. 'But not till I get back. I want to hear it.'

Venables stretched out a long arm and tapped Ovey on the shoulder. 'The pen is yours, sir,' he croaked, 'you have won it nobly.'

He disappeared leaning on Mr Rules's arm, and 3R sprang up and burst into speech. 'Super story, Ovey.' 'Yer, smashing story, weren't it?' 'Is it a giant squid, Ovey, is it?' 'Put us in the story, Ovey, we could fight the headhunters.' 'Oh, Ovey, put me in the story, *please*.' 'We didn't want them old parrots, Ove, we wanted to tame a shark!'

They streamed away, babbling and bubbling. 'Old Wilkes with that leaf on 'is 'ead,' chortled the Dodgy Boys.

The Egg-Shaped Boy

Ovey remained alone in the classroom, an egg-shaped boy standing on an island. For a moment longer he stood there, hearing the distant surge of praise, basking in the warmth of popularity, dazzled by success. Then he put the pen in his pocket, turned, and, presently, plunged again into the pouring rain and went home, talking and laughing to himself as he worked out the ending to the story of *The Instant Island*, that 3R wanted and only he, Ovey the Storyteller, Ovey the Magicmaker, could give.

Charlie Plans a Maths Lesson
Sylvia Woods

'I'm going to be a landlady,' said Mrs Robinson.

'What's a landlady?' asked Charlie, who was scraping up the last of his cornflakes.

'I know,' said Lucinda. 'You let rooms to people.'

'But we haven't any spare rooms,' said Charlie.

'There's Gran's room,' said his mother. 'I'm letting it for three weeks to a student teacher who is coming to your school for teaching practice. She was going to stay at the farm, but Mrs Ford is booked up with summer visitors, so I said we'd have her.'

'Is a student teacher someone who's learning to teach?' asked Lucinda.

'Yes,' said Mrs Robinson. 'Now have you finished, you two? It's time to get the car out.'

As soon as they arrived at school Lucinda ran off to tell her girl friends in the Top Juniors, where Sir taught, all about the student who was going to stay with them. Charlie joined the

Lower Juniors who were racketting about in the lobby and swapped his Cadbury's Flake with Tim Winters's Mars Bar before Miss Clarke called them into the classroom. She sat at her desk collecting dinner money as she did every Monday morning. When she had taken Charlie's envelope, she told him to go and tidy the Nature Table.

'It's your turn today, with Robert,' she reminded him.

Charlie and Robert were friends. They liked the same things and hated the same things. One of the things they hated was doing the Nature Table.

'Nature's silly,' said Robert.

'All flowers and growing beans and mustard and cress and all that muck,' said Charlie.

There were eight pots of very dead flowers and the blotting paper had dried up round the runner beans. The bell for assembly rang before they finished, so they left the flowers to droop still lower in their jars and filed out with the rest of the Lower Juniors into Sir's class.

As Charlie passed the piano, he managed to trip Lucinda who was putting the hymnbook on its stand. She fell on to the keys and made a massive crash of discords that sounded like Stravinsky. 'Carefully, carefully,' said Sir, who hadn't seen exactly what happened.

Lucinda glared at Charlie, but he was looking

the other way.

After prayers and a hymn, Sir told them about the student, and Charlie pricked up his ears.

'. . . she will be coming on Thursday to visit the school and get to know us. Then she will return to college, but later on she will be back for three weeks to do some teaching. I am sure you will do your best to make her welcome and that I can count on all of you not to let yourselves down by bad behaviour.' He paused to look hard at a few of the Lower Juniors, and Lucinda knew which ones he was looking at.

'Right,' he said, 'Lower Juniors, return to your class.'

Back in the Lower Juniors' classroom the place buzzed with excitement because Miss Clarke said that the student was going to teach them. There was even more excitement when Charlie announced that the student would be staying in his house.

'Cor . . . I wouldn't like a teacher staying with me. Oh, sorry Miss Clarke,' said Annie Thomas who always put her foot in it. 'Why can't she go on living at the college?' she went on quickly.

'Because it's thirty miles away and too far for the coaches to get them all out to country schools like ours in time to be here at nine o'clock,' explained Miss Clarke.

Thursday came and their student arrived in a minibus. Her name was Miss Thompson and she and the Lower Juniors spent the morning getting to know each other. Annie Thomas thought she was 'ever so nice' and Carole Davies liked the way she did her hair. Charlie hated her. It was all because she asked to look at his English book. His English book was very private. He knew he couldn't spell and so did Miss Clarke, but he didn't see why he should let Miss Thompson into the secret.

'Where's your English book, Charlie?' she asked.

'Dunno,' said Charlie.

'Well, it can't be far, can it?' She began poking around in Charlie's drawer.

Charlie stopped her. 'I'll look,' he said. He messed about in his drawer, turning books over and over and hoping she would go away. By mistake, the English book came up on top and before he could send it to the bottom again, Miss Thompson pounced.

'There it is,' she said, and sat on his table turning the pages. At last she handed the book back. 'Thank you, Charlie,' she said. She opened her notebook and wrote a few things in it. All that Charlie could see was his name at the top of the page, then lots of writing he couldn't manage to read. She was probably writing about how dumb he was.

'What are your hobbies?' she asked, after she had been writing for a bit.

'I dunno,' said Charlie.

If Miss Thompson had asked him what things he most liked doing, he would have known what she meant. He could have told her about fishing from the bridge with Robert and Tim, about collecting spiders and stones and shells and sticking pictures of his favourite pop stars into a scrapbook. But she didn't ask him that.

'Do you like reading?' she asked.

'No,' said Charlie.

'Do you like anything?' asked Miss Thompson.

'Spiders,' said Charlie, and he was going to tell her about his collection of super whoppers in the tool shed at the bottom of the garden when she turned away.

'She's daft,' said Robert, who had been listening in.

'I hate her,' said Charlie. 'I wish she wasn't coming to live with us.'

When Miss Thompson came to stay later in the term, Mrs Robinson arranged for all the family to have a meal together in the evening. Charlie didn't say a word all through supper, although his mother tried to include him in the conversation. Miss Thompson had lots to say to his mother and father. She made them laugh when she told them funny things that happened at college. She talked about the college tutors as well. These were the teachers whose job was to show the students how to teach. There was one she was really afraid of. Her name was Miss Follyfoot. She taught at the college and went out to schools to watch her students teach. If she thought they weren't good enough, they had to leave college and find a different job.

On the way to school in the car next morning, Lucinda was very talkative. She described how the school was run by Mr McKay, 'Sir' to everyone except the teachers, and what the classes were like. The Top Juniors were the best, the Infants weren't bad, for babies, and the Lower Juniors, in spite of having a good teacher, were the end and she was sorry for Miss Thompson. Charlie glared but said nothing.

Miss Thompson didn't take the whole class for lessons during the first week, she taught only the top group, but she used to read a story to the class at the end of each day. She read about Robin Hood and sometimes let them act bits of it and she chose Charlie to be Robin. Charlie grudgingly admitted to himself that she wasn't bad, and by the end of the week, he wished he was in the top group. They were doing all sorts of unusual things with Miss Thompson. They visited the church and went to the top of the tower with Mr Patterson the vicar. Then they went round the graveyard to look at the tombstones to find out which were the oldest. Twice they sat on the pavement outside the school and did traffic counts and one afternoon, Miss Thompson took them across to the village shop to buy flour, sugar, margarine, raisins and candied peel to make rock buns.

Charlie began to like Miss Thompson. She told him one day at breakfast that Miss Follyfoot had discovered some wrong spellings in her notebook.

'Can't you spell either?' asked Charlie.

Miss Thompson grinned. 'Not always,' she said.

Charlie could see that she was terrified of Miss Follyfoot and each time her tutor came everything went wrong, even with Miss Clarke and all the top group willing it to go right.

It made Miss Thompson very miserable. 'She never comes to the good lessons,' she told Charlie's mother.

'You must stop being afraid of her,' said Mrs Robinson. 'Forget about her. Pretend she's not there.'

'I can't,' said Miss Thompson. 'As soon as I see her I go all tight inside. I know everything will go wrong and it does.'

During her second week in school, Miss Thompson taught the whole class and they loved it. But they could be sure that if a science experiment failed to work or if paint water was spilt or an important book went missing, it would happen when Miss Follyfoot was there. At the end of the second week, Miss Follyfoot said she was coming in on the following Wednesday morning and she was bringing the Principal of the college with her.

'That must be because I'm so awful,' Miss Thompson told the Robinsons at tea time. 'The Principal hardly ever goes out to see students unless there's something wrong with them.'

'What are you going to teach when they come?' asked Mrs Robinson.

'She says I've got to do a maths lesson,' said Miss Thompson. 'I don't know what I shall do. Most of the class are doing individual work and need lots of help.'

'Do something they can all manage,' Charlie heard Miss Clarke say to Miss Thompson the next day. 'Like measuring. The top group understand about radius and diameters, so let them measure bicycle wheels on Wednesday, and they can try to find out about circumferences. The middle group can have the big tape measures for doing perimeters and areas. Now the lower group *are* a bit of a problem . . .'

Then Miss Clarke noticed Charlie. 'You get on with your work card, Charlie,' she said. 'Miss Thompson will be with you in a moment.'

On Friday evening, Miss Thompson began making a set of sum cards which the lower group could use the following Wednesday. Charlie watched her and thought they were very dull. Each card had two coloured lines of different lengths drawn on it. The lines were labelled A and B. Each card had a sentence which said: 'Measure line A and line B. Which line is longer and by how much?'

'Even the dumbies in the lower group will be bored out of their minds doing those,' said Charlie when he and Robert met in the Robinsons' tool shed later that evening.

'Well we can't do anything about it. She'll have to fail, that's all,' said Robert.

'She can't fail. It wouldn't be fair,' said Charlie. 'She can teach all right when Miss Follyfoot isn't there.'

'Couldn't we capture her and tie her up and put her in the Boiler House?' suggested Robert.

'Then she'd be sure to fail if she was tied up and

couldn't teach,' objected Charlie.

'Idiot,' said Robert. 'I mean tie up Miss Folly-foot.'

'She's too big,' said Charlie. 'Haven't you seen the size of her feet and those long dangling arms? She'd clobber us before we got the rope out and anyway, she's bringing some Sir with her who runs the college.'

'All right,' said Robert, 'so what shall we do?'

Charlie thought. 'Measuring wheels and the playground's all right. It's the sum cards which are going to fail her. We've got to do something about those sum cards.'

'What?' asked Robert.

'I dunno,' said Charlie, 'but they ought to be jazzed up a bit.'

The tool shed was gloomy and Charlie went outside. He leant against the side of the shed and put his hands in his pockets and scuffed the ground with one foot. Robert followed him out and they both crouched on the path to watch a couple of worms wriggling in the dust near Charlie's feet.

'Got it!' yelled Charlie, springing up and nearly trampling on the worms in his excitement.

'Got what?' asked Robert.

'The sum cards,' said Charlie. 'Instead of measuring lines, they can measure worms.'

'It's much more difficult measuring worms,' said Robert. 'They don't keep still, especially if you try to line them up with a ruler.'

'That's all right,' said Charlie. 'Maths is supposed to be a difficult subject.'

'Where do we get the worms?' asked Robert.

'Dig,' said Charlie. 'There must be a million in this garden.'

'We'll need to keep them somewhere till Wednesday,' said Robert.

'In matchboxes,' said Charlie. 'I've got heaps upstairs.'

Robert started digging for worms while Charlie ran indoors for his matchboxes.

'I've got thirty-seven,' he announced, coming back with a bulging plastic bag. 'Let's get thirty-seven, all sizes.'

It took some time, but at last, thirty-seven worms lay in thirty-seven matchboxes. Then it was bed time, so they left the boxes in the shed under the work bench hidden beneath plastic sacks.

On Saturday Charlie brought out his felt-tipped pens so that they could write numbers on the boxes. Later in the day they begged a couple of pieces of coloured card from Miss Thompson and took them to Charlie's bedroom, where they cut them into thirty-seven cards. It was hard work and the writing took them all the rest of the day with pauses for meals. Charlie looked through them when they had finished.

'They'll have to do,' he said.

'Your writing's all lop-sided,' said Robert.

'Yours is like a spider's with a hang-over,' said Charlie. 'Let's have a look at the worms.'

The worm in the first box they opened looked dead, even when Charlie poked it.

'What's wrong with it?' asked Robert.

They opened a few more boxes and all the worms in them looked as bad as the first.

'They were all right when we put them in,' said Charlie. 'I remember number twenty-eight especially, he was a fighter. Look at him now.'

He flicked worm twenty-eight and it didn't

trouble to squirm. It lay there where his finger had put it.

'They'll be dead by Wednesday,' said Robert. 'Fancy making all those cards for nothing.'

'I know what's wrong,' said Charlie, 'They're drying up. Do you remember in the Infants? We put them in a wormery because Mrs Bray said that worms need to keep damp.'

'We can't wet the matchboxes, they'll rot,' said Robert.

'They'll have to go in my old aquarium,' said Charlie, 'With lots of damp earth. I'll get up early on Wednesday morning and put them back in their boxes. I always hear Miss Thompson's alarm.'

They found the aquarium and put the worms in it and thanks to Miss Thompson's alarm clock Charlie managed to get the worms reboxed before breakfast on Wednesday. They had all survived after their spell in the wormery except number twenty-eight which Charlie decided was clinically dead and threw out of the window.

In school everyone could see that Miss Thompson was nervous. Miss Clarke reminded them that Miss Follyfoot was coming with another visitor from the college and asked them to be on their best behaviour. It was a very hot day, so the lower group took their tables and chairs to a shady part of the playground so that Miss Thompson could keep an eye on them while she was with the other two groups who were doing their practical work.

They had arranged themselves outside when a car drew up and Miss Follyfoot got out with a grey-haired, jolly-looking man and they went in together to see Sir. Miss Thompson gave out her sum cards to the lower group and explained what they had to do. She sent the middle group to start measuring the playground and then settled down with the top group who were measuring bicycle wheels. 'Come on,' said Charlie.

He and Robert went over to the lower group who were busily measuring lines A and B at their tables under the big chestnut tree. Out of the corner of his eye, Charlie saw Miss Follyfoot and the Principal come to the school door. Robert was already collecting in Miss Thompson's cards and giving out the ones he and Charlie had made.

'You can work in twos if you like,' said Charlie as he handed round the boxes, 'and there are more cards and boxes,' he added, putting the spares on the ground beside Annie's table.

'Charlie and Robert, aren't you supposed to be measuring the door?' said Miss Thompson.

They hurried towards it and stepped politely aside as Miss Follyfoot came down the steps.

'It's all right,' she said. 'Go on with what you are doing. I've only come to watch. What are you . . .' She stopped because a scream of terror from Annie Thomas came across the playground, followed by more screams from Carole Davies. There was sudden uproar from the whole lower group. Johnnie Norbut started to chase Susan Carter round the playground with two worms dangling from his fingers. Annie Thomas stood on her chair and Carole Davies demanded Miss Clarke at the top of her voice. A table was knocked over and Jenny Biggs was having hysterics screaming that Christopher Dodds had dropped a worm down her dress.

Sir, Miss Clarke and Mrs Bray collided in the doorway as they came to see what had happened.

'Hey!' yelled Charlie. 'Stop treading on those boxes. You'll kill the worms.' He ran over to where Johnnie Norbut was jumping up and down in front of Susan Carter who was crouching behind the overturned desk and screaming blue murder.

'Get your foot off those boxes!' shouted Charlie.

'You shut your mouth,' yelled Johnnie, giving Charlie a thump in the eye.

Charlie landed a punch on Johnnie's nose and it began to bleed.

Johnnie kicked Charlie and then the two of them rolled over and over on the ground until they were lifted off each other by the Principal and Sir.

Charlie shook himself as well as he could while

he was still being gripped in the Principal's firm hand. Then the school and the playground and the chestnut tree stopped whizzing round and everybody came back into focus. Miss Thompson looked as if she was going to cry. Charlie didn't want to cry. He was mad. Mad with Johnnie Norbut for running about chasing people with worms instead of measuring them. Mad with the whole of the lower group for messing up the lesson and making Miss Thompson fail.

When order had been restored, it was Miss Follyfoot who asked Sir to let Charlie explain, and the Principal seemed as interested as she was to hear his story. From the look in Sir's eye, Charlie knew that he wanted to slipper both him and Johnnie Norbut so hard that neither of them would be able to sit down comfortably for a week. But Sir had to be polite to visitors, so he sat and listened while Charlie told them how Miss Thompson had thought that Miss Follyfoot was going to fail her and how he and Robert had worked so hard all weekend to make the lesson a success.

When he had finished, Sir punched his hands together. 'Well I'm da . . . er, well I'm blessed,' he said, and forgot all about slippering people.

The Principal was laughing and Miss Follyfoot had a grin on her face which made her look quite human. The Principal looked at Miss Thompson. 'If you can inspire such devotion in your pupils, you can't be that bad,' he said. 'Don't worry. No one's going to fail you.'

Miss Follyfoot turned to Charlie and Robert. 'It was very kindly meant,' she said. 'But I think you had better let teachers plan their own lessons in future.' Her face changed. 'You weren't thinking of being teachers yourselves when you grow up?'

'No, Miss Follyfoot,' said Robert and Charlie in horror.

'Thank goodness for that,' said Miss Follyfoot.

A Hallowe'en Happening
Margaret Joy

Everyone in Miss Mee's class was very busy. It was Hallowe'en, and they were decorating the classroom with scary things.

Jean and the twins Barbara and Rosemary were cutting out black cats and then sticking bright green paper behind to shine through the eyeholes. The cats were going to go up on the windows.

Ian and Michael were cutting out big fat spooky shapes and making large eyeholes: they were going to be masks. Ian tried one over his face and scared Mr Loftus, who was just passing the window with a ladder.

Paul and Pete had already painted some white skeletons on black paper and now Miss Mee was hanging them from the ceiling, where they swayed and danced.

Wendy, Nasreen and Asif had painted egg-boxes black, and now they were twisting on hairy black pipe-cleaners for legs – these were going to hang from the classroom ceiling *just* inside the door. 'When one of these brushes against someone, I bet they nearly jump out of their skin!' said Asif.

Brenda, Imdad and Sue were making black-crêpe paper clothes for some dolly pegs. They were going to be witches with pointed black hats and wild hair made out of bristles from the classroom brush.

Little Larry was talking to himself as he drew things to go into a spell: 'An eyelash and an egg and an owl's feather . . .'

Outside the windows of the classroom, the sky seemed to be growing darker as great grey clouds rolled overhead. The wind was whistling round the corner of the school and coming in through the cracks between the windows. It made the skeletons shiver and tremble on their strings.

Miss Mee climbed down off the table and put some music in the tape recorder. It was music they liked to listen to in the hall: first the clock striking twelve, then the skeletons coming to life and dancing, slow at first, then faster and faster and wilder and wilder until the cock crew and the skeletons melted away into the morning mist.

'It's the skelly music,' said the children, pleased, but they were glad the classroom lights were bright and they were all together.

The music was very faint; the clock had just finished striking and the first skellies were

stretching and walking on tip-toe before they started to dance.

'A toe-bone and a finger-bone,' said little Larry, still drawing his spell. The children listened to the music growing faster.

Suddenly, they all stopped work and looked round with big eyes. There was a strange noise: a loud thumping, like giant footsteps, then a lo-o-o-ong scraping noise and a short scream. Every-one – Miss Mee too – heard the dreadful sounds and held their breath. The loud creaking giant footsteps began again, then gradually died away.

The wind whistled even more loudly outside;

now the skellies were dancing madly to the music, and the painted skellies were swaying and turning with them, grinning their great white painted grins. Everyone was sitting very quiet, forgetting their work. 'A flitty bat and a creepy spider,' murmured little Larry.

Click! The lights went out, suddenly. Everyone gasped. The classroom was quite dark. No one moved. Miss Mee quickly reached into her drawer for the birthday candle and the matches. She stood the candle in its holder on her desk. Its white flame quivered. 'Aaaahh . . .' said everyone, watching it and feeling better.

The cock crew very faintly and the skellies began to tip-toe away with the music and disappear.

Click! Without any warning the lights came back on. Everyone started to chatter and smile again. 'Buttercups and daisies and silver stars,' said Larry, still drawing.

Mr Loftus opened the classroom door and a black spider brushed against him. Everyone laughed loudly, but Mr Loftus didn't laugh at all. He came over to Miss Mee looking very stern and holding a football boot between his finger and thumb.

'Just look what some joker threw up on the roof,' he said. 'I expect you heard me up there just now. The boot was jammed in the television aerial. I gave it a good tug and cut my hand on the wire – my, that made me yell!'

'Poor Mr Loftus,' said Miss Mee, and she fetched the plasters.

'The lights went off,' said Wendy.

'Yes, that was while I was mending the aerial,' explained Mr Loftus. 'I had to switch off at the mains for a minute.'

He looked round at everyone. 'You weren't worried, were you?'

'No, oh no, course not . . .!' cried everyone quickly. But the painted skellies swayed and nudged each other, grinning their wide, white grins. *They* knew.

Marmaduke

Barbara Ireson

The china teapot lid, patterned with roses, lay on the kitchen floor in two pieces. Katey was standing near the breakfast table looking at it. Her lower lip trembled and her eyes filled with tears.

'It's Marmaduke's fault,' Katey cried as her mother came into the room. 'He dropped it. He's a naughty boy. He shouldn't have touched it.' Tears streamed down her cheeks. She tried to brush them away with the sleeve of her green woollen jumper.

Katey's mother sighed. It wasn't the broken teapot lid. It was Marmaduke.

It had all begun a few weeks ago when they moved to Ishford and Katey changed schools. As soon as she got home after her first day at the village school Katey started to complain about a boy called Marmaduke. Marmaduke had made her talk during a lesson and her new teacher, Miss Price, had been cross with her. Marmaduke had made her drop her lunch in the playground and it had been too dirty to eat. Marmaduke had made her knock over her paint jar and her painting was spoiled. Mrs Bates listened and thought Marmaduke sounded rather a rough boy. She hoped he wasn't going to bully Katey.

That evening, while Mrs Bates was upstairs drawing the curtains in the bedrooms, Katey spilled her cocoa all over the white rug in front of the television in the sitting room. 'Marmaduke jogged my elbow,' she told her mother as she tried to mop up the mess with her handkerchief. It spread into a big brown pond of a patch and the more she rubbed the worse she made it.

It was then, as Katey began to cry and her tears

flooded down into the chocolatey mess, that Mrs Bates realized Marmaduke did not exist. Katey had made up Marmaduke. She was blaming an imaginary boy for things she did herself.

Mrs Bates fetched a bowl of hot soapy water from the kitchen and cleaned the rug. She helped Katey to undress and put on her nightgown. She read her a bedtime story as she always did, but she didn't say a word about Marmaduke.

She thought about him, though. She thought about him a lot when Katey was asleep and she was sitting knitting. She decided that Katey was not happy at her new school. She needed time to settle down. Mrs Bates made up her mind to listen patiently to everything Katey had to tell her about school and take no notice of what she said about Marmaduke.

For a few more days Marmaduke got the blame for lost shoes, lost pencils, torn books, wrong spellings and tumbles in the playground. Then, gradually, Katey stopped talking about him. Until this morning when the teapot lid was broken, Katey had not blamed Marmaduke for anything for a whole week. That was why Mrs Bates sighed. She was sorry to hear his name again.

She fetched Katey's school coat from the hall and helped her to put it on. She did up the buttons and gently wiped Katey's face with a tissue. 'You do like your new school now, don't you, Katey?' she asked.

'Yes,' Katey hiccupped between sobs.

'And you are getting your spellings right, aren't you?'

'Yes,' mumbled Katey, sniffing and wiping her nose on her coat sleeve.

'And you like your new teacher, don't you?'

'Miss Price is lovely,' whispered Katey, still weeping.

'Well then, stop crying. I'll mend the teapot lid. You'll see, it will be just like new when you come home at teatime.'

Katey sniffed and buried her face in her mother's arms. Mrs Bates looked at the clock on the kitchen wall. 'It's a quarter to nine,' she said. 'Time we were on our way to school.' She bent down and kissed Katey on the cheek. 'Pick up your lunch from the table.' They went down the garden path and out of the gate.

The Bateses' new house was at one end of the street and the school was at the other end. Gate after gate opened and children came out to go to school. A girl with long hair shouted, 'Hello Katey,' as she pedalled along on a bicycle.

'Hello!' Katey whispered. 'That's Sally James,' she told her mother. 'She's in my class.'

'Do you know the names of all the children in your class now?' asked Mrs Bates.

'No, only a few. I know Sally because she sits at my table. I know Henry because he's got red hair. I know Malcolm because he's rough.'

When they got as far as the railings where the school playground began, Katey said, 'I can go on my own now.' She stood on tip-toe, gave her mother a peck of a kiss, and skipped off nervously. The playground seemed vast to her, but she had to cross it to get to the school door. She zig-zagged to avoid being bumped into by the big boys who were chasing about. A football bounced up in front of her, but it missed her, and she ran on.

Children were crowding through the door. They all seemed big to Katey, and she was carried along with them. As she reached the door of her classroom, a shoe flew over her head. She edged in, squeezing past two boys who were swopping badges. Malcolm leaped down from his chair with a fearsome warcry, lost his balance and fell against Katey, stepping heavily on one of her feet. 'Sorry, Katey Batey,' he called out as he flung his arms round the boy who was throwing shoes. They fell struggling to the floor.

Katey stood nervously near the table where she usually sat. She felt bewildered by the noise. 'Can we squeeze past?' asked Henry with red hair. He was holding a plastic dish in the air above his head. Sally James was behind him carrying another. 'We're going to fetch the gerbil's food and water,' Henry shouted above the din. 'Make sure no one opens the cage while we're away.' They forced their way out into the corridor.

The gerbil's cage was in a corner of the classroom near a window, and the door was shut. The gerbil poked its nose between the bars and Katey stroked it. She was glad to be there where it was quieter. She watched the gerbil climb into its wheel and begin to send it round and round. In a few minutes Sally came back and carefully put the dish of water into the cage without spilling it. But Malcolm got up just as Henry passed, and knocked the seed dish out of his hand.

Henry raised his hand to thump Malcolm but someone caught it and held it firmly in the air above his head. It was Miss Price.

'Class Two!' she cried. 'Class Two! Quiet!'

She waited until there was no noise at all and then said, 'Go to your places without another word.'

When every table was straight, every chair upright and every boy and girl still, she said, 'What has come over you, Class Two? I just can't believe my class was making such a row. It's not like you at all. You're usually so well-behaved. That's what I was just telling this new boy.' She stretched out her hand to a boy who had been standing behind her. He had dark hair and was dressed all in blue. Katey liked the way he looked. Blue jumper, blue shirt, blue jeans and blue sneakers.

'These eighteen noisy boys and girls are Class Two,' she told him. 'Last term we were only seventeen, but Katey Bates joined us about three weeks ago. Katey knows how it feels to be new, so she'll be good at looking after you.' Miss Price walked over to the table where Katey was sitting and said, 'I think we can make room for you next to her.' She picked up a spare chair. 'If you move along towards the end of the table, Katey, I can get this chair in for Marmaduke.'

Katey just stared at her. Marmaduke! She didn't move.

'Hurry up, Katey,' said Miss Price.

Katey was looking at the boy all dressed in blue who was called Marmaduke.

'This is all I want you to do, Katey,' explained Miss Price. She picked up Katey and her chair and moved them both together. 'There,' she said, pushing in the other chair. 'Come here, Marmaduke. This is your place now.' Marmaduke squeezed in and sat next to Katey.

At four o'clock Mrs Bates went to meet Katey from school. Usually she met her about half-way along the street, but today she had almost reached the playground railings before she saw Katey coming. 'You're a late Kate today,' she said, smiling and holding out her hand.

'Marmaduke wanted to choose a library book, so I stayed behind to help him,' Katey told her, still buttoning up her coat as she walked along.

Mrs Bates said nothing, but she wondered if something had gone wrong at school. Then, remembering how upset Katey had been at breakfast-time, she said, 'I've mended the teapot lid. It's just as good as new now.' But Katey seemed to have forgotten all about it. All she wanted to talk about was the gerbil. 'I made sure he didn't get out of his cage,' she told her mother, 'and tomorrow Sally says I can fetch the water with her.'

While her mother was cutting bread and butter for tea, Katey drew a picture of the gerbil in his cage, and after tea she drew a picture of Miss Price in the pink dress she'd worn to school. There was a boy all dressed in blue in the picture too.

When her mother kissed her goodnight, Katey mumbled sleepily, 'My milk spilled all over the floor this morning. It wasn't my fault. Marmaduke knocked it over. His chair was too close to mine. Miss Price wasn't cross at all. She put him there.' Katey turned to the wall and closed her eyes.

Mrs Bates switched off the light. She stood in the doorway in the dark, feeling uneasy and puzzled. She was sure Katey was settling into her new school happily now, so why was she talking about Marmaduke again?

She went downstairs and looked up Miss Price's telephone number. She dialled . . . six . . .

one . . . three . . . nine . . . then she stopped. 'It doesn't seem fair to disturb her in the evening,' she thought. 'I'll give Katey another day or so.' She sat down in a big comfortable chair and watched television and would not let herself think about Marmaduke.

'It's my turn to give out the paint pots today,' Katey told her mother as she crunched her way through a huge bowl of crispy cereal. 'Miss Price says I can fill them all by myself so I must get to school early.' There was still warm tea left in her mug, but she got down from her chair and ran to fetch her coat. 'Can we go now, Mummy?' she asked, bringing her mother's coat too.

As they hurried along she said, 'Look, there's Sally in front. I'll run on now,' and then she added, 'Before I put out the paint I want to sharpen my red and yellow crayons. Marmaduke broke them yesterday.'

Mrs Bates wished she'd telephoned Miss Price after all. Then she noticed that she'd forgotten to give Katey her lunch. When she got to the school gates, Katey had already crossed the playground.

'Excuse me, please.' A small dark boy was trying to get past her.

'I'm sorry,' she said, stepping inside.

The boy looked about the same age as Katey, but she couldn't remember having seen him before. 'Would you mind taking this lunch in for me?' she asked.

'I'm new,' he told her. 'Yesterday was my first day at this school. I don't know anyone yet.'

'It's for someone in Class Two. It's for Katey Bates.'

'That's all right then. I'm in Class Two.' He took the lunch packet. 'I know Katey. I sit next to her.'

'Thank you,' said Mrs Bates, 'and what's your name then?'

'Murphy,' he called back as he ran across the playground. 'Marmaduke Murphy.'

Mrs Bates watched him until he disappeared through the school door. Now she understood. There really was a new boy, Marmaduke Murphy, who had spilled Katey's milk. And Katey had stayed behind after lessons to help him choose a library book. And he had broken the red and yellow crayons Katey had just hurried in to sharpen.

When Katey sat down to tea after school that afternoon, there was a poem on her plate in her mother's writing. This is what it said:

> *Marmaduke Murphy, who sits next to Kate,*
> *Was told by her mother inside the school gate,*
> *'This is Kate's lunch. She left it behind.'*
> *So he took it in to her. Wasn't that kind!*

From that time on the only Marmaduke that Katey ever talked about was Marmaduke Murphy. And he became her best friend.

BOSS OF THE POOL
Robin Klein

The last thing Shelley wanted was to have to spend her evenings at the hostel where her mother worked, because she wasn't allowed to stay in the house on her own. Then to her horror, mentally-handicapped Ben attaches himself to her and although he's terrified of the pool, he comes to watch her swimming. Despite herself, Shelley begins to help him overcome his fear. A compassionate story of the growth of an unlikely friendship.

MATILDA
Roald Dahl

Matilda is an extraordinary girl, sensitive and brilliant. But her parents are gormless, and think Matilda is just a nuisance and treat her as a scab, to be endured until the time comes to flick her away. As if this isn't enough, she has to cope with the odious headmistress, Miss Trunchbull. When Matilda is attacked by Miss Trunchbull one day, she suddenly discovers she has an extraordinary power which can make trouble for the monstrous grown-ups in her life.

NOW THEN, CHARLIE ROBINSON
Sylvia Woods

Charlie Robinson is always full of ideas, whether he's trying to liven up a maths lesson, solve the mystery of noises up a chimney or turn the Nativity Play into a really special event. His exploits at home, at school and out and about in the village make very entertaining reading.

STAN

Ann Pilling

Running away from his London foster home, Stan unwittingly gets caught up with vicious criminals and is pursued by one of them. But throughout his terrifying journey to Warrington and Liverpool and then by ferry across the Irish Sea, he never loses the hope or the determination to find his brother and the home he dreams of.

TORCH

Jill Paton Walsh

Dio and Cal had gone to ask the old man for permission to marry. Instead, Dio finds himself commanded to be the Guardian of the Torch in the old man's stead. Without quite knowing why, they embark on an extraordinary journey, bearing the Torch in search of the Games! And in doing so they learn some of the secrets of the Torch and of the mysterious past time called 'Ago', a time of wonderful machines, now lost forever.

CRUMMY MUMMY AND ME

Anne Fine

How would you feel if your mother had royal-blue hair and wore lavender fishnet tights? It's not easy for Minna being the only sensible one in the family, even though she's used to her mum's weird clothes and eccentric behaviour. But then the whole family are a bit unusual and their exploits make highly entertaining reading.

A LITTLE LOWER THAN THE ANGELS
Geraldine McCaughrean

God, the Devil, Heaven and Hell all stand before Gabriel's eyes – he can scarcely believe them. But when he is forced to flee from his cruel master, the stonemason, and leaps into the smoking jaws of Hell, he discovers a new and exciting life. But will his life with the travelling mystery players be any more secure than his old one? In a world of illusions people are not always what they seem. Least of all Gabriel.

SON OF A GUN
Janet and Allan Ahlberg

A galloping, riotous wild west farce in which the plot thickens with every page until a combined force of Indians, U.S. cavalry, old-timers, dancing girls and the 8-year-old hero are racing to the rescue of a mother and baby beseiged in their cabin by two incompetent bandits.

THE BIG PINK
Ann Pilling

Straight from her friendly local comprehensive Angela is plunged into the alien life of her aunt's boarding school for girls. Overweight and horribly self-conscious she immediately attracts the disapproval of Auntie Pat and the suspicion of the girls in her dormitory. But slowly she finds allies, and her secret talent wins her the admiration of the teenage grandson of the school's benefactor . . .